Foolish Fishgirls and The Pearl

Barbara Pease Weber

A SAMUEL FRENCH ACTING EDITION

SAMUEL FRENCH

FOUNDED 1830

SAMUELFRENCH.COM
SAMUELFRENCH-LONDON.CO.UK

FOOLISH FISHGIRLS AND THE PEARL premiered under the working title *The Pearl* at Theatre West in Lincoln City, Oregon in in July 2012. The performance was directed by Stina Seeger-Gibson, with assistance from Paul Wilhelmi, and set by Bruce Jackson, Jr. The cast was as follows:

CORAL . . . . Debbie Hendrickson
OCEANA . . . . Cindy Wesolowski, Stina Seeger-Gibson
MARINA . . . . .Lisa Austin
FLOYD. . . . . Bryan Kirsch
SHEILA . . . . .Idaliise Putansu
PEARL. . . . . Roseanne Murphy
NATHAN . . . . .Don Shufflin

FOOLISH FISHGIRLS AND THE PEARL (under its working title) was then produced at Iron Mountain Stage Company in Ringwood, New Jersey, in December 2012. The performance was directed by Petra Seirmarco. The cast was as follows:

CORAL . . . . Linda Handzus Gerdes
OCEANA . . . . Patricia Baran-McNair
FLOYD. . . . . .Jack Burger
SHEILA . . . . .Patty Sullivan
PEARL. . . . . Laura Moskin
NATHAN . . . . Salvatore Seirmarco

FOOLISH FISHGIRLS AND THE PEARL (under its working title) fwas then produced at The Old Academy in Philadelphia in February 2014. The performance was directed by Helga Krauss: The cast was as follows:

CORAL . . . . .Catherine DeRemigio-Fichera
OCEANA . . . . .Loretta Lucy Miller
MARINA . . . . Michelle Loor Nicolay
FLOYD. . . . . .Robert Toczek
SHEILA . . . . .Michelle Moscicki
PEARL. . . . . .Lauren Jones
NATHAN . . . . Ivo Becica

CHARACTERS

(In order of appearance:)

CORAL – (late 40s/early 50s) A flat broke, snowbound, middle-aged former mermaid and co-owner of Sea Hags, a ramshackle bed and breakfast at the New Jersey seashore.

FLOYD – (mid-50s/early 60s) A breakfast patron of Sea Hags. Maybe one day he'll have it in bed!

OCEANA – (late 40s/early 50s) Coral's sister and co-owner of Sea Hags. She's also a broken hearted former mermaid. After all, misery loves company! That's what sisters are for!

MARINA – (late 40s/early 50s) Coral and Oceana's hoity-toity former mermaid cousin. That is, until *the Captain* dumps her when her treasure runs out!

SHEILA – (40s/50s) The town Police Chief, Dog Catcher, L&I Inspector, Public Works Commissioner, and Justice of the Peace. Of course she can do it all! She's a woman!

PEARL – (early 20s) The new "maid" in town. She doesn't say much. But, she doesn't have to. She's a buck-naked knockout!

NATHAN – (mid 20s/early 30s) A handsome young Coast Guard Lieutenant who should have had two hands on the wheel when driving over a bridge! He will next time!

SETTING

Early January in the off season at *Sea Hags*, a rustic bed and breakfast/café in desperate need of repair, somewhere at the New Jersey seashore, owned and and managed by spinster sisters, Coral and Oceana, who live on the premises.

TIME

When gasoline prices are high and the economy is in the tank.

For John,
With oceans of love and whales of laughter,
xoxo
Barbara

ACT I

Scene I

*(AT RISE: Sounds of squawking seagulls are heard on this cold and overcast morning. **CORAL** enters from the upstairs apartment and begins to ready the café for opening. She yawns, groans, scratches and stretches as she turns on the radio, puts on a pot of coffee and places sugar containers on the counter and tables. She then goes offstage right into the kitchen. There is a Closed sign on the door. After the radio news report concludes, **FLOYD** Ferguson, bundled in an old parka, scarf and hat and gloves and carrying the morning newspaper, arrives at the café door, hungry for his breakfast. He stops outside the door, turns his back, reaches into his coat pocket and pulls out breath spray. He spritzes his mouth a couple of times before attempting to enter.)*

(Oldies music fades to advertisement and news report: "WJPW News and Weather for Monday, January third is brought to you by The Captain and his lovely wife, Marina, at Island Savings and Loan. Don't capsize your credit in a choppy sea of debt! Call Marina today and make an appointment to sit down with The Captain who'll help you to pay off those holiday bills with a home equity line of credit from Island S and L. Experience smooth financial sailing with The Captain, Marina and the rest of the crew at Island Savings and Loan. The Jersey shore is going to be

hit with the first storm of the New Year as a Nor'Easter with up to ten inches of snow and freezing rain makes its way through the region. Snow, heavy at times, is predicted to begin falling at shortly after daybreak. Stay indoors if you can and if you can't, buckle up and drive safely. The Seaspray Bridge is closed due to road work following an accident late last evening. Use the Belfast Causeway as an alternate route to travel to and from the mainland. And now, back to more continuous music from the oldie but goodiest station on the island, WJPW."

(Oldies music returns in light of the previous "paid advertisement" by the Captain and **MARINA** *then fades as* **FLOYD** *attempts, unsuccessfully, to enter.)*

FLOYD. *(Attempting to open the front door to the café only to find that it is locked. He looks at his watch, knocks politely a few times and waits patiently to no avail, then proceeds to bang loudly.)* I know you're in there. I can smell the coffee brewing.

CORAL. *(Poking her head out of the kitchen.)* We're *CLOSED!*

FLOYD. Let me in, Coral. It's freezing out here.

CORAL. Move to Miami!

FLOYD. Open up!

CORAL. *(Coming out of the kitchen.)* I open at *six, Pinky.*

FLOYD. It *is* six.

CORAL. *(Points to her watch.)* It's *five* to. *(She goes into the kitchen.)*

FLOYD. *(Banging.)* If you don't appreciate my business, I'll take it elsewhere.

CORAL. *(From kitchen.)* Go right ahead. I'm tired of seeing your ugly mug first thing in the morning.

FLOYD. Where's Ana? She lets me in. At *ten* to.

CORAL. It's *my* morning to open. And I open at *six*. Not *ten* to. Not *five* to. Not *one* to. At Six. S. I. X. *Six!*

FLOYD. *(Leaving in a huff.)* I don't know why I come to this dump in the first place.

CORAL. 'Cause this is the *only* dump on this lousy *island* where you can get a decent cup of coffee in the off season.

FLOYD. *(Retorting.)* Ana makes better coffee anyway. Yours tastes like somebody took a p…

CORAL. *(Cutting him off.)* Watch it, Pinky. Or I might accidentally drop the pot in your lap next time.

FLOYD. There won't be a next time. And, stop calling me *Pinky!* *(We hear his truck door slam and him drive away.)*

*(**OCEANA** enters from the upstairs apartment.)*

OCEANA. *(Unlocking the door and flipping the sign on the door from Closed to Open.)* You scaring off the customers again?

CORAL. Only Pinky Floyd. He'll be back when he remembers that Dockside is closed for the month of January.

OCEANA. *(Looking out the window at the sky.)* Weatherman says we're supposed to get snow. Eight to ten inches.

CORAL. *(Dismally.)* What a way to start the New Year. Flat broke and snow bound in South Jersey.

OCEANA. I hate being broke. But I do love the snow.

CORAL. You won't when the pipes freeze.

OCEANA. *(Wistfully.)* There's nothing more beautiful than a snow-covered beach.

CORAL. I wish we could afford to close for the winter like the other businesses on this rinky dink island.

OCEANA. You'd think being the only game in town we'd have more customers. If Floyd doesn't come back we may not get a single sale today.

CORAL. He'll be back. He's cold and hungry.

OCEANA. Wish there were more like him around.

CORAL. Smelly old geezers?

OCEANA. Paying customers!

CORAL. You making chowder today?

OCEANA. Did Mario deliver the crabs?

CORAL. They're on ice out back. He trapped some beauties.

OCEANA. *(Looking out the window.)* Look, it's starting to flurry.

CORAL. *(Yawning and stretching.)* We may as well close up now and go back to bed. Until June. *(She flips the sign to Closed.)*

OCEANA. *(Flipping sign back to Open.)* Nonsense. I have a feeling that today is going to be special. A fresh snow fall to welcome in a brand new year. *(She takes a cleansing breath.)* Can't you just smell it in the air? Like when we were young and carefree and spent all of our free time splashing around in the waves.

CORAL. You been watching those sappy old movies again?

OCEANA. Not much else to do around here in the winter.

CORAL. You can say that again. *(She goes into the kitchen.)*

OCEANA. *(She picks up a broom and starts to sweep. After a beat, she looks out the window.)* Oh no. What's *she* doing here?

CORAL. *(From kitchen.)* Who?

OCEANA. The *Empress of Foreclosure Isle.* Get a load of that limo.

CORAL. *(Coming out of the kitchen and looking out the window.)* Guess *Toe Nail* didn't want to tarnish her new Jaguar with a couple of snowflakes.

OCEANA. Look at that coat. She looks like she got swallowed up by a bear.

CORAL. *(Flipping sign to Closed.)* She probably wants money. Quick! Hide! *(She scampers behind the lunch counter and ducks for cover.)*

OCEANA. Too late. She saw us. *(She flips sign back to Open and continues to sweep the floor.)*

> (**MARINA,** *glamorously dressed in chic winter boots, a fur coat, fur hat and leather gloves, enters.*)

MARINA. Good morning, *Sea Hags*! Am I too early for coffee?

OCEANA. Well, well, well. You're out of your shell awfully early this morning, Marina. To what do I owe this honor?

MARINA. I just thought I'd drop by to wish you and your *charming* sister a Happy New Year!

OCEANA. At six in the morning?

MARINA. And, to get a cup of coffee, for *the Captain,* if you don't mind. Black. To go.

OCEANA. *(Pointing outside to limo.)* That's some ride you have out there. I'm surprised it doesn't come with a coffee bar.

MARINA. It does, of course. Yet, for some reason which I cannot fathom, *the Captain* prefers *your* swill.

OCEANA. Well, tell *the Captain* we're flattered.

MARINA. Of course you are.

OCEANA. So, where's the new Jag? Did you tire of it already and trade up for a limo?

MARINA. We're supposed to get some snow today and *the Captain* doesn't want to chance driving. *The Captain* and I are heading into the *city.*

OCEANA. *(Pouring coffee.)* Well, that sounds like fun. Give *the Captain* my regards. *(She hands* **MARINA** *a Styrofoam cup of coffee.)*

MARINA. I shall. *The Captain* is the limousine on a *video conference.*

OCEANA. *(Unimpressed.)* My goodness. That sounds important. I hope you trimmed his nose hair.

MARINA. *(Ignoring the quip.)* You can't see him, of course, because the limousine windows are *tinted. (The limo horn blows impatiently and* **MARINA** *turns and waves out the window.)* I'll be right out, *Captain! (To* **OCEANA,** *trying to "spin" the angry horn blast.)* Isn't that sweet? I'm only gone one minute and *The Captain* already misses me.

OCEANA. Then you should go! Quickly!

MARINA. *The Captain* is conferring with our attorneys. The *Captain and I* are taking possession today of five more beachfront properties right down the street. We'll practically be neighbors!

OCEANA. *(Sarcastically.)* I can't wait!

MARINA. Which reminds me, Oceana. Although I hate to mix business with *(Holding up the Styrofoam coffee cup.)* *pleasure,* I feel as though since I'm already here I must remind you that you and your sister are very late with several payments on your line of credit. It is *January* already you know. *The Captain* is becoming increasingly concerned about your ability to pay.

OCEANA. Coral and I are well aware of our payment obligations, Marina. You'll have your money. After all, wouldn't want you and *the Captain* to go hungry. End of the month. At the latest.

MARINA. Darling, that's what you said *last* month.

OCEANA. I admit, business has been a bit slow. It *is* the off season. And, we didn't anticipate having to repair roof until next year. But we had no choice. It was about to collapse after the storm in October and would have damaged the fourth floor guest rooms.

MARINA. I know. That *is* a shame. And I keep reassuring *the Captain* that you and Coral are good for the money that our bank so generously loaned you to renovate your quaint Bed and Breakfast. *(She looks around.)* Although, from the looks of it, you haven't made any progress, have you? Of course, I'd be completely distraught if *the Captain* and I were forced to file a lien against you and Coral for non-payment and ruin your credit. We *are cousins,* after all. We did grow up together. Which is also why I'm here. Where is the *other* Sea Hag? I need to speak with both of you.

OCEANA. Coral went into town. Picking up supplies.

MARINA. *(Dismissively.)* She did not. I saw her running for cover as I was coming up the walk. By the way, you really should be a bit proactive and throw down some ice melt out front. The snow is starting to come down. You don't want to risk a slip and fall. Your insurance will go sky high. *(Calling.)* Coral! Come out, come out wherever you are! You can't hide from me forever you know.

> *(***CORAL*** *pops up from behind the lunch counter wielding a butter knife and a bottle of Bacardi.* ***MARINA*** *shrieks and spills coffee on her coat.)*

CORAL. *(Imitating a drunken Pirate.)* Ahoy, Matey! Yo-ho-ho and a fifth of Bacardi! Rub a dub dub. Thirty clams in a tub. *(She hands* ***MARINA*** *the butter knife and waves a white napkin.)* Here. Take my silver dagger. I *surrender.* To *the Captain and Toe Nail.* No more torture! Please! Go ahead. *(Offering the butter knife.)* Slit my throat from ear to ear. *(She lays her head, face up, on the lunch counter as if on the chopping block.)* Stick an apple in my mouth and serve my head on a silver platter to *the Captain* with a side of caviar. You can have it "to go" in your stretch limo and feast on my eyeballs on your way to *the city.* Go ahead, Toe Nail. I'm worth more dead than alive. You can do the honors. Just, do me one favor, and make it quick.

MARINA. *(Blotting her coat with a paper napkin.)* See what you made me do? It's going to cost a fortune to have this coat cleaned. Honestly, Coral! Grow up!

CORAL. What do you want, *Toe Nail?* Besides the silver in my teeth?

MARINA. I wanted to wish the both of you a Happy New Year. But I don't know why I bother.

CORAL. Me neither.

MARINA. And, I would really appreciate it if you would desist referring to me as *Toe Nail.* It's disgusting.

CORAL. I would. But, you know what they say. If the sandal fits…get a pedicure.

MARINA. You're impossible. All right. I'll get to the point. Not to dredge up ancient history or unpleasant memories or hard feelings or anything. Yours, not mine, that is…

OCEANA. What makes you think we have hard feelings, Marina? Do *you* have hard feelings, Coral?

CORAL. Absolutely not, Oceana. Why should *I* have hard feelings?

MARINA. Of course, you don't. Well, anyway, I was just wondering, and I know this is going to sound a bit unusual, but I was wondering if…this morning…when you woke up…either of you happened to notice…

> *(Loud impatient horn blasts from limo outside – The Captain is not pleased that **MARINA** is dallying.)*

> *(Waving to window.)* I'm coming, Captain! *(More horn blowing.)* Here I come. *(Distraught that she has upset The Captain.)* Oh my.

CORAL. What are you blathering about?

MARINA. *(Having second thoughts.)* Nothing. Never mind. I have to go. *(Fake cheerful.)* Mustn't keep *the Captain* waiting! He is utterly *lost* without me!

CORAL. I'll buy him a compass.

MARINA. Ha. Ha. You should do stand up.

CORAL. How would you know? When all you do is *lie down?*

MARINA. Watch it, Coral. Or you'll be…

CORAL. Or I'll be *what?????*

> *(More angry horn blasts from the limo.)*

OCEANA. *(Ushering her to the door to avoid bloodshed.)* Well, have fun in the city, Marina. Thanks for stopping by.

MARINA. Oh, don't worry about that, Oceana. We *will.* *(Exiting, to **CORAL**.)* And, I'm sending *you* the cleaning bill for this coat!

CORAL. *(Shaking her head.)* What a piece of work!

OCEANA. Indeed, she is.

CORAL. Are we really related to *that?*

OCEANA. Indeed, we are.

CORAL. *(Imitating* **MARINA.***)* "*The Captain* is utterly lost without me!" Give me a break.

OCEANA. I hate to admit it. But, of the three of us, Marina turned out to be the smart one.

CORAL. *(Frustrated.)* That's what absolutely drives me *bonkers!* Not so much that we were foolish. We were young. Dumb. In *love.* Ha! Love! But, the fact that *Marina* was the clever one is sometimes more than I can bear.

OCEANA. Let it go.

CORAL. I try. But it's hard to let it go when she rubs it in our face all the time. *(Imitating* **MARINA.***)* "*The Captain* is on a video conference." "*The limo* has tinted windows." Arrgh! *Toe Nail* is living large in the lap of luxury while we can't even afford to make a couple of renovations on this ramshackle B&B without going into hock on a loan from *the Captain* that I have absolutely no idea how we'll be able to repay.

OCEANA. Ignore her and she'll go away. Or at least not come round as much.

CORAL. Ha! Not when we're on the proverbial hook to her and the Captain for the money we borrowed. If we don't pay up they'll take our business. Then we'll not only be out of a job – we'll be out of a home.

OCEANA. You call our tiny apartment upstairs a home?

CORAL. You heard her. Their taking possession of five more properties. Down the street. Pretty soon they'll own the whole island.

OCEANA. I think that's their master plan. Though I'm not sure why they'd want it.

CORAL. They're cooking something up. They probably want to tear down our property and build something else. Why else would they have been so eager to give the two of us a loan if not to foreclose on us?

OCEANA. We'll find a way to pay them back.

CORAL. How? Are you expecting money to fall from the sky? Or, have you finally figured out how to recover buried treasure from the ocean floor?

OCEANA. Wouldn't *that* be nice? *(She looks out the window to the sky.)* If only snowflakes were dollar bills. We'd be zillionaires. It's really starting to come down. *(She points.)* Look. Floyd's coming back.

CORAL. Told you he would.

OCEANA. Don't be so sure. Floyd could very well have gone to Crabby Clem's across the bridge. They're open.

CORAL. Nah. Floyd's a creature of habit. Besides, I heard on the radio that the bridge is out. So if Pinky wants his breakfast he either eats with us or he goes hungry. He's been here nearly every morning since he moved to this crummy island couple of years ago.

OCEANA. That's right. Floyd moved here shortly after his wife died. So be nice. He's still in mourning.

CORAL. Okay. I'll only put *one* laxative in his prune juice this morning.

OCEANA. Coral!

CORAL. Just kidding. *(Exiting mumbling under her breath.)* He's getting a double dose.

> **(FLOYD** *enters carrying a newspaper, mad as a hornet, and sits at a table and takes off his coat and hat.)*

OCEANA. Morning Floyd.

FLOYD. Your *sister!*

OCEANA. *(Pouring him coffee.)* You can only choose your friends, Floyd.

FLOYD. How do you stand to work with that woman *every* day let alone live with her?

OCEANA. I'm fine, Floyd. Thanks for asking. *(Pouring him a cup of coffee.)* Juice today?

FLOYD. She is so infuriating!

OCEANA. Apple it is.

FLOYD. You know, I would have gone over to Clem's for breakfast, but the bridge is out.

OCEANA. What'll it be today? Your usual? Or the special?

FLOYD. And Dockside is closed all month. The Garrisons went down to South Carolina.

OCEANA. The usual. White, wheat or rye?

FLOYD. I'm going to start making my own darn breakfast!

OCEANA. You betcha. Two scrambled eggs, whole wheat toast and a side of grits.

FLOYD. It's barely twenty degrees outside and *she* wouldn't open the door five stinkin' minutes early. What does she expect me to do? Sit it my truck with the heat on burning gasoline while she counts down the seconds? Where does she think she is? NASA?

OCEANA. Happy New Year, Floyd.

FLOYD. *(Coming to.)* Oh. Why, thank you, Oceana. Same to you. Let's see now. *(He studies the menu which of course he knows by heart.)* I'll have…two eggs scrambled with a side of grits. And white toast. No. Make that wheat.

OCEANA. Coming right up.

FLOYD. And, I think I'll have apple juice today instead of prune.

OCEANA. Wise choice. *(She exits to the kitchen and* **FLOYD** *puts on his glasses and glances at the newspaper.)*

FLOYD. *(Calling into the kitchen.)* Snowing outside. Nor'Easter blowing in.

OCEANA. *(From kitchen.)* I know. We got that new roof on just in time. Now all we need are some guests to fill the rooms upstairs.

FLOYD. Bridge is out over by Crabby Clem's.

OCEANA. I heard. What happened?

FLOYD. Bad accident. Bridge must have been icy. Car careened into the bay in the middle of the night. Took out a whole section of guardrail and some piling.

OCEANA. Hope nobody got killed.

FLOYD. Water's awful cold.

OCEANA. That it is.

FLOYD. Search and rescue out there now. Looking for a body.

OCEANA. Oh dear. Nobody we know I hope.

FLOYD. Dunno.

OCEANA. Is it in the paper?

FLOYD. Probably tomorrow.

> *(Justice of the Peace, Mayor, Police Chief, Dog Catcher and all around town municipal maven,* **SHEILA** *Karpinski, enters.)*

SHEILA. Brrrrr! Jeepers, it's cold as a witch's tit out there. Morning Floyd. Happy New Year.

FLOYD. Morning Sheila. Happy New Year to you too. We were just talking about the accident on Seaspray Bridge. (**SHEILA** *looks around. Sees nobody. Shrugs.*)

SHEILA. How've you doing, Floyd? Staying out of trouble?

FLOYD. Don't have much choice in the off season. Not much trouble to find in this town, Ms. Mayor. Or, are you the Justice of the Peace today?

SHEILA. (*She opens her jacket to display an assortment of badges pinned to the inside. She points to the badge du jour.*) Don'tcha see my badge? I'm Police Chief today. Yesterday I was Dog Catcher.

FLOYD. You're a regular Jackie of all Trades.

SHEILA. Just like you, Floyd.

FLOYD. I can fix a thing or two if I put my mind to it. My wife, rest her soul, used to say I was the Jack**ass** of all Trades. Confounded woman. Always calling me names.

SHEILA. Ha! She had way with words, huh?

FLOYD. She sure did.

SHEILA. What's it been? Couple years now? Since you moved out here on the island?

FLOYD. Marilyn passed two years last week and I've been here ever since. Couldn't stand the thought of being alone in that empty house. Trouble is, no matter where

I am, there…here… I miss her just the same as the day she… *(He can't finish.)*

SHEILA. *(Pats his arm.)* I know. It's hard to be alone. Which reminds me. Yesterday, when I was the Dog Catcher, I caught me a stray Golden Retriever don'tcha know.

FLOYD. You don't say? Where?

SHEILA. I was on patrol, up on the north shore. I caught him rummaging through trash cans looking for food. I took him home. Fed him a couple of hamburger patties and some rice. Larry cleaned him up, and if we can't find a good home for him we just may decide to keep him. Although our house really isn't large enough for a third mutt. Hey, any chance you'd be interested in a Golden Retriever? He's down right loveable. And, he's lonely, same as you. You should think about it, Floyd. He'd be great company.

FLOYD. Ah, I… I don't know, Sheila.

SHEILA. Okay. Well. You think about it and let me know. He's awful sweet. All right?

FLOYD. Sure. All right.

*(**CORAL** enters from kitchen with **FLOYD**'s food.)*

CORAL. *(Sarcastically, thumping a breakfast plate on the table in front of **FLOYD**.)* Thought you weren't coming back.

FLOYD. You knew that bridge is out and you let me drive away anyway. With the price of gas these days. You should be ashamed of yourself.

CORAL. If you're so worried about fuel costs why do you drive a gas guzzling jalopy?

FLOYD. My truck is none of your business. And she's not a jalopy!

CORAL. Then don't complain to me about the price of gas.

FLOYD. I'll complain about the price of gas to whomever I want to complain to about the price of gas!

CORAL. Well, I'm not listening. *(She plugs her fingers in her ears then sings.)* La la la. La la la.

FLOYD. What's the harm of letting me come in, sit down and read my newspaper two minutes early?

CORAL. If I let you in two minutes early then I have to let everybody else in two minutes early!

FLOYD. Wasn't nobody outside but me!

CORAL. I don't want to set a precedent.

FLOYD. Of all the foolishness I ever heard. What kind of a business you running around here? I'm a regular customer and you let me drive away.

CORAL. You could have waited two minutes. You got real far didn't you? Stubborn old fool.

FLOYD. You could have opened up the door. Miserable sea witch.

CORAL. It's not my problem that you're an insomniac. The only way you're getting in here before six is if you're wearing an apron and peeling potatoes.

FLOYD. Gimme a sharp knife and I'll show you what I can peel.

CORAL. What a big bad tough guy you are… *(Taunting.)*… *Pinky*!

FLOYD. Don't call me *Pinky*!

OCEANA. *(Entering from kitchen.)* Would you two knock it off already? *(to* **SHEILA***)* Morning Chief. How about performing a great public service and arresting these hooligans? They're causing a disturbance in my café. In fact, why don't you lock 'em up in the same cell. Then we can take bets on who kills who first.

SHEILA. I would, Oceana, but then I'd be the one stuck with cleaning up the carnage. I'm also on Public Works this week. Harold's out with the flu. I'll tell you what, though. *(She takes our her "ticket book" out of her jacket pocket.)* I'll write them both a hefty citation instead. For being a public nuisance.

OCEANA. Perfect!

SHEILA. May I use your rest room?

OCEANA. Of course. Coffee?

SHEILA. Yes, please. To go. Large. Cream and sugar. Got to get back to the bridge. Bad accident. *(She exits offstage left to restroom.)*

(Sirens are heard.)

CORAL. *(Going to window to look outside.)* There goes an ambulance. Maybe they found a body.

OCEANA. Dead or alive do you suppose?

FLOYD. Since it's an ambulance, probably alive.

OCEANA. I hope so!

CORAL. No way. It is a low bridge but that water is way too cold.

FLOYD. They wouldn't need an ambulance for a dead body.

CORAL. How would they cart it away? On a dog sled?

FLOYD. I bet he's alive.

CORAL. Why do you automatically assume it's a man? Could be a woman.

FLOYD. I wasn't talking to you.

CORAL. *(Snarling with a near empty coffee pot coffee ominously over **FLOYD**'s lap.)* More coffee?

OCEANA. It doesn't matter if it's a man or woman. I just hope whoever it is lived.

*(**SHEILA** comes out of the bathroom.)*

SHEILA. In the bridge accident? It's a young man.

FLOYD. *(To **CORAL**.)* Told you.

CORAL. Thought you weren't talking to me.

OCEANA. *(Holding **SHEILA**'s take out cup.)* Then he lived?

SHEILA. By the grace of God.

OCEANA. Who is it?

SHEILA. I can't release the name yet – have to contact his family first.

OCEANA. Is he a local?

SHEILA. Nope. Coast Guard. Returning from holiday leave. To the base down in Cape May.

OCEANA. Alone?

SHEILA. Seems that way.

FLOYD. Drinking?

SHEILA. They're not ruling out anything at this point. He may have fallen asleep at the wheel. He's hallucinating. At least he was when he came to. Probably from the freezing temperature. Or gulping too much ocean water. *(She takes coffee cup from* **OCEANA.***)* What do I owe you?

OCEANA. Don't be silly. On the house.

SHEILA. Thanks.

OCEANA. Hallucinating. That's not a good sign, is it?

FLOYD. What's he seeing? The ghost of Elvis or something?

SHEILA. The rescue team found him on the beach. Covered up to his neck in a mound of sea grass. Which undoubtedly insulated him from the cold and saved his life. When he came to, he told one of the rescuers that he hit an icy patch on the bridge and his car spun out and went over the guard rail. He remembers sailing over the side of the bridge and splashing into the water. Then everything went pitch black. He was trapped in his car and it was sinking fast. And just before he passed out from the shock of the icy water he said that he saw a vibrant light coming toward him, and as the light got closer he realized that it was a beautiful *mermaid,* glowing with an aura of the most radiant colors he had ever seen. The mermaid somehow got him out of his car and swam with him in her arms up to the surface and to the shore. Then, she laid next to him on the beach and breathed air back into his lungs. He said she gave him the sweetest kiss he ever had and he felt safe and warm in her arms as he fell fast asleep.

> *(***CORAL*** and ***OCEANA*** are mesmerized by ***SHEILA****'s story. As ***SHEILA*** finishes, ***CORAL****'s mouth is wide open in astonishment and she drops the coffee pot in ***FLOYD****'s lap scalding him and then the pot bounces off and spills all over the floor.)*

FLOYD. Watch it with that pot! You tryin to scald me woman?

> (**OCEANA**, *equally shaken by the tale, tries to remain composed and springs to action to clean up the mess.*)

OCEANA. It was just an accident. You're fine Floyd. Coral didn't mean it. Breakfast on the house today.

CORAL. *(Shaken.)* He said *what?*

SHEILA. The young man said that the mermaid must have covered him up with the sea grass after she kissed him because the next thing he knew was that he woke up as the rescue team was covering him with blankets and giving him oxygen.

CORAL. *(She sits, shaken.)* I don't believe it!

OCEANA. *(Covering.)* You're right, Coral. That's quite a hallucination! See what prolonged exposure to the elements can do to a person!

SHEILA. Well, I gotta head back to the bridge. I get to spend the rest of my day sitting in my car in front of the bridge with my lights flashing so nobody crosses it. Thank goodness for crosswords and Sudoku. Hope Frank Mayfield can take the graveyard shift. If not, I'll be calling you, Floyd. How'd you like to get deputized and spend the night in loser cruiser with the lights flashing? I know a nice mutt who'd love to keep you company.

FLOYD. Not especially. But call me if you get stuck. Is this a paying job?

SHEILA. The best kind. Under the table. Petty cash.

FLOYD. I don't have to do Sudoku do I? Never did get the hang of it.

SHEILA. You can pass the time however you want. So long as it's *legal*, that is,

FLOYD. You're on then.

SHEILA. Great. I'll call you if Mayfield bails on me. *(To* OCEANA.*)* Thanks again for the coffee. See you later.

FLOYD. So long, Sheila. Keep warm out there.

OCEANA. Yes. Stay warm, Sheila. Happy New Year.

CORAL. *(Still in shock over* **SHEILA***'s story.)* Ana! Do you know what this means?

OCEANA. *(Avoiding* **CORAL***'s question.)* Oh my! Look at the snow coming down. I think you're absolutely right, Coral. We should close for the day. Hunker down. Keep warm. No sense boiling those crabs for chowder. They'll keep till tomorrow. Probably nobody will venture out in this weather. *(Handing* **FLOYD** *his check and hat.)* Here's your check, Floyd. Be careful driving home.

FLOYD. Hey! I thought you said it's on the house. Since your sister here tried to get me to sing soprano with scalding coffee.

CORAL. It was *lukewarm.* Last of the pot. You sissy.

OCEANA. You're absolutely right, Floyd. On the house! Here, let me help you on with your coat.

FLOYD. I'd like another cup of coffee if you don't mind. This time in my *cup!*

CORAL. Too bad. Pot's broken. Now get outta here. Scram!

FLOYD. You treat your customer's like seaweed and you'll be out of business in no time. Talk about the bum's rush.

OCEANA. *(Wrapping his scarf around his neck and putting his hat on his head.)* I'm sorry Floyd. This weather is making me nervous. Come back tomorrow. When the weather's better.

FLOYD. There's barely an inch out there.

OCEANA. Oh no. It's at least two or three. *(Pushing him out the door.)* Drive safely. *(She locks the door and puts the Closed sign on the window.* **FLOYD** *bangs on the door.)*

FLOYD. *(Perturbed.)* My newspaper!

> *(***OCEANA** *scurries back to the table, grabs his newspaper, hurries to the door, opens it and throws it at him.)*

OCEANA. Here! *(She slams door and pulls down the shade.)*

CORAL. *(In a state of shock.)* You *know* what this means, don't you?

OCEANA. We can't be sure!

CORAL. Oh, yes we *can!*

OCEANA. There's no way.

CORAL. Oh really?

OCEANA. Let's not jump to conclusions. He hallucinated. The ocean is ice cold!

CORAL. How did he get out of his car?

OCEANA. He swam out!

CORAL. With the windows closed?

OCEANA. Maybe his window was open.

CORAL. In *January?*

OCEANA. *(Thinking of rational explanation.)* He *could* be a smoker.

CORAL. When a mermaid saves the life of a sailor, she can choose to spend the rest of her life on land.

OCEANA. Only if they fall in love.

CORAL. Baloney. What fairy tale have you been reading?

OCEANA. That's how it works!

CORAL. That's *not* how it works. That's just what they want you to *believe.*

OCEANA. Who?

CORAL. In the movies. No box office bonanza if they told the *real* story. That the sailor turns out to be…

OCEANA. *(Cutting her off.)* We don't even know that the young man is a *sailor!*

CORAL. You heard what Sheila said. The boy is in the *Coast Guard!*

OCEANA. That doesn't make him a *sailor!*

CORAL. It sure don't make him a *cowboy!*

OCEANA. I know, but…

CORAL. When is the last time you heard of something like this happening?

OCEANA. You're jumping to conclusions!

CORAL. Answer me!

OCEANA. Coral, get hold of yourself.

CORAL. I'm asking you a question! When is the last time something like this happened? A mermaid rescuing a sailor from drowning in the sea?

OCEANA. Pick up the *National Inquisitor.* You can read a new mermaid story every week. Right next to the other hogwash about aliens, ghosts, genies, and witches.

CORAL. You're avoiding my question, Oceana. A mermaid rescuing a handsome young sailor from the sea off the shores of New Jersey? When was the last time you heard tell of such a thing?

OCEANA. I… I…

CORAL. *WHEN?????*

OCEANA. *(Blurting it out.)* When **WE** did it! ***You, me* and *MARINA*!** Thirty years ago!

    (blackout/curtain)

Scene II

(*SETTING: Same. Later that morning.*)

(*AT RISE: The snow is falling hard with several inches of accumulation.*)

OCEANA. (*Entering from front door brushing off snow, wearing ski jacket, boots hat and carrying a snow shovel. As she is placing shovel against the wall and brushing off snow from her jacket,* CORAL *hobbles out of the kitchen with a snorkel in her mouth, wearing sea goggles, a one piece bathing suit [with optional cover up – preferably open], a swim cap, winter leg warmers, scuba fins/flippers, and a winter scarf. She carries a beach towel.* OCEANA *turns and sees* CORAL.) Where the *hell* are you going in *that* get up?

CORAL. (*Taking snorkel out of her mouth.*) To the beach!

OCEANA. Are you out of your mind? It's twenty degrees outside. Put some clothes on!

CORAL. I am! (*She exits to offstage closet to retrieve her boots, hat, gloves and coat and proceeds to bundle up, boots first, to prolong the outlandish effect of winter wear over beach attire.*)

OCEANA. Planning to get a jump start on your suntan?

CORAL. I'm going to the bridge.

OCEANA. It's closed. You heard Sheila. She's standing guard. You can't get across.

CORAL. I'll pull to the side. Go out to the jetty.

OCEANA. The rocks are surely covered with ice. You'll fall in.

CORAL. It's not like I forgot how to swim!

OCEANA. You can't swim with a broken neck!

CORAL. She's out there! I know she is! Waiting for the sailor to come back. To find her. I've got to get to her first.

OCEANA. He's in the hospital. He's not coming back.

CORAL. They always come back. Then they leave you. With a broken heart and two skinny legs.*

> (*Alternative language depending on the actress playing **CORAL**.: "With a broken heart and two pudgy legs.")

OCEANA. Maybe it won't happen the way it did with us.

CORAL. We can't take that chance.

OCEANA. Why should we even care about some starry-eyed mermaid who we don't even know?

CORAL. She's probably a blood relative!

OCEANA. Of course. You're right.

CORAL. She's out there. Can't you feel it?

OCEANA. From the moment I woke up this morning, I could feel it. Her. Something. But, maybe she's long gone by now. If she was watching she probably saw the ambulance take him away.

CORAL. She's biding her time. Don't you remember? That's what *we* did.

OCEANA. You're wasting yours. You'll never find her. Unless she wants you to.

CORAL. I have to see for myself.

OCEANA. See what? There's nothing to see.

CORAL. If she's out there, and I call her, she'll hear me. And, she'll come.

OCEANA. I don't want her to come! She needs to stay where she is!

CORAL. It's too late for that.

OCEANA. Not if we warn her!

CORAL. Why should she listen to us?

OCEANA. We have experience. We know what it's like.

CORAL. What? That the ocean always looks bluer from the other side.

OCEANA. Exactly.

CORAL. *We* were warned.

OCEANA. I know, but…

CORAL. *(Cutting her off.)* Did *we* listen?

OCEANA. I listened. To *YOU.*

CORAL. You listened to *me?* Please! You listened to the sweet nothings that blue eye'd sailor whispered in your ear. I didn't force you to stay.

OCEANA. I wasn't going back without you.

CORAL. You should have. Two wrongs don't make a right.

OCEANA. Would you have gone back without me?

CORAL. We should have both gone back. And left *Toe Nail* here. With *the Captain.* Ugh.

OCEANA. Living "happily ever after."

CORAL. Marina may be rich. I'll give you that. However, she's anything but happy.

OCEANA. She makes a pretty darn good show of it.

CORAL. If it wasn't for the buried treasure Toe Nail has stashed away *the Captain* would be long gone. She spoon feeds it to him, gold coin by gold coin, just to keep him around.

OCEANA. Like I said, *she* was the smart one.

CORAL. Nah. She's slowly dying inside. Marina knows when the last of the treasure is gone, so too, is the Captain.

OCEANA. *(Looking out the window.)* You really think the mermaid is still swimming out by the bridge?

CORAL. What's the old saying about returning to the scene of the crime? The fair maiden may even be ashore by now. She may have even begun to transform.

OCEANA. Do you think she *did* it?

CORAL. What?

OCEANA. Splashed water on the bridge. Made it icy. So the boy's car would go over the side and she could nab him.

CORAL. It's possible.

OCEANA. If he *is* a sailor, maybe she's had her eye on him for a while.

CORAL. No doubt, she's a clever one.

OCEANA. I remember how *you* were at that age.

CORAL. You weren't so innocent yourself.

OCEANA. I didn't 'cause that shipwreck! You and Marina did!

CORAL. *(With nostalgic reflection.)* That tsunami was pretty awesome, wasn't it?

OCEANA. Your best work.

CORAL. Thank you.

OCEANA. *(Raising a coffee cup to toast the achievement.)* To the victor, go the spoils.

CORAL. Except, unfortunately, the spoils seem to have stayed with Marina. Aaarrgh!
How could we have been that stupid? Not to have held anything back for ourselves. Like she did.

OCEANA. *Marina* broke the rules. *We* didn't.

CORAL. Marina may have broken the rules but we're the ones paying the price. How do you suppose that is?

OCEANA. Look on the bright side. We rescued forty seven souls that day, including women and children.

CORAL. Not to mention a couple of good for nothing Merchant Marines, who, in retrospect, we should have let drown.

OCEANA. *(Nostalgically.)* Hans and Fernando.

CORAL. Ugh. What were we thinking?

OCEANA. Hindsight is always twenty-twenty.

CORAL. What could we possibly have seen in those two?

OCEANA. *(Reminiscent, dreamily.)* Hans had blond hair, blue eyes and a boatload of charm. He was Norwegian.

CORAL. *(Longingly.)* Fernando was *Venezuelan.* He had brown eyes, dark wavy hair, and a grrrreat big…

OCEANA. *Smile?*

CORAL. Among *other* things.

OCEANA. With age comes wisdom.

CORAL. Which is why I've got to get to the newbie before it's too late. You know, I sometimes wonder.

OCEANA. What?

CORAL. What if, you know, we *didn't* fall head over fin in love with Fernando and Hans?

OCEANA. Not a day goes by when I wish we hadn't.

CORAL. Fernando pledged his undying love to me. He called me his "Ocean Princess." How was I supposed to know he already had a wife and four kids in Venezuela? He should have been wearing a wedding ring!

OCEANA. Hans *was* single. I'll give him that.

CORAL. *(Dryly.) Hans* was *gay.*

OCEANA. *(Defensively.)* Hans said he *loved* me too. When all along he was only after my treasure. And, right after I handed it all over to him, lock, stock and pirate's chest, he broke the news. *(Imitating Hans with a Norwegian accent.)* "Ana," he said, "I must tell you." " I'm very gay!" What did I know? I thought he meant I made him happy.

CORAL. You made him happy all right. You made him downright ecstatic. He took off with *your* treasure chest.

OCEANA. And, Fernando and his wife and four kids in Venezuela are living happily ever after with *your* treasure chest.

CORAL. *(Spilling the beans after 30 years.)* Fernando *wasn't* my first choice, you know.

OCEANA. *(Stunned.)* You never told me that!

CORAL. Before I rescued Fernando, I had my eye on a *different* sailor.

OCEANA. Really!!!???

CORAL. Yes. What a sorry twist of fate that turned out to be.

OCEANA. Didn't you get to him in time? Did he *drown?*

CORAL. No. No! He made it. *I think.*

OCEANA. You *think?*

CORAL. I'm sure he did. See, as I was in the process of rescuing my first pick – him – a handsome young American, whose long, lean arms were wrapped around my slender neck as I swam him away from the sinking ship, he caught a glimpse of his ship mate who couldn't swim and was going down for the third time. The young American pleaded with me to save his friend, *Fernando,* from drowning. So, I scooped up a piece of drift wood that was floating nearby and I helped the young sailor to climb on it. Before I gave him a good shove toward the shore, I plucked the gold and emerald pendant from my necklace and put it in his pocket so he would have something to remember me. I watched the young sailor drift safely to shore as I scooped up Fernando. And, I'll never forget. As the handsome American was floating away holding tight to the drift wood, he turned to me and shouted over the crashing waves, "Thank you for your kindness, beautiful Angel of the Sea. I'll never forget you." *(Shaking her head in disappointment over the one that got away.)* I wonder whatever happened to that sailor? That boy could have turned out to be my one true love. I bet *he* didn't have a wife and four kids. *(Sighs.)* Although he probably does by now. *(Gathering her things.)* Well, *c'est la vie.* I'm off to the bridge.

OCEANA. I'm going with you.

CORAL. No. You should stay here.

OCEANA. Why?

CORAL. In case she shows up!

OCEANA. Who?

CORAL. The mermaid!

OCEANA. Why would she come here? It's not like we have a sign outside "Mermaid Motel – Swim In and Put Your Fins Up."

CORAL. She can probably sense us. Mermaid pheromones. Better sensory perception than dolphins.

OCEANA. That's it! When I woke up, the air smelled different. Familiar. More pungent. It must have been her. I just didn't recognize it. It's been so long I'd practically forgotten the sensation. I bet Marina noticed it too. That's what she wanted to talk to us about.

(Phone rings, **OCEANA** *answers.)*

Sea Hags, best chowder on the island. Oh, Hello Floyd.

CORAL. *(Grabbing phone from* **OCEANA** *and shouting into it.)* We're CLOSED!

OCEANA. *(Grabbing back the phone.)* Sorry, Floyd. The weather has her out of sorts today. Really? *(To* **OCEANA.***)* Forecast changed. They're now predicting a foot and a half.

CORAL. *(Now bundled up in outer gear over swimwear.)* Hang up. Are you coming with me or not?

OCEANA. Why, that's very kind of you, Floyd. I don't know. What do you think? Three bags? Or four? *(To* **CORAL.***)* He's picking us up some salt. For the sidewalk.

CORAL. *(She rolls her eyes.)* I'm leaving.

OCEANA. *(To* **CORAL.***)* Wait one second! *(To phone.)* If you wouldn't mind, Floyd, put the salt in the storage room in the back of the kitchen. I'll leave the door unlocked. Uh, in case we're not here when you come. Ah…well, we have to run an errand. I know it's a blizzard outside. But…we need to go out…ah…to…the pharmacy! We need medicine. Yes, I know the roads are bad…but… we have…uh…we have a *toothache!*

CORAL. *(Cringing.)* We have a toothache?

OCEANA. *(Into phone.)* That is, I have a toothache. Coral needs her prescription filled. No! No thanks. We have to go ourselves. Because it's a…personal medication. For her feminine problem. She's sensitive about it. You understand. (**CORAL** *shoots her a "you've got to be kidding me" look.)* Thanks anyway, Floyd. We'll be careful. Just put the salt in the back room. Bye now.

CORAL. A "personal" medication for my "feminine" problem? What am I? Undergoing a sex change? Why couldn't I be the one with the toothache!

OCEANA. I couldn't very well tell him the truth! Why else would we being going out in the middle of a blizzard if it wasn't for drugs?

CORAL. To buy a shovel! *(She points to the snow coming down.)*

OCEANA. *(Pointing to shovel by the door.)* We have a shovel!

CORAL. He doesn't know that!

OCEANA. If he's already getting us some salt, don't you think he could pick us up a shovel too!

CORAL. Oh, never mind!

OCEANA. Oh! That reminds me! *(She runs upstairs to the bedroom offstage.)*

CORAL. *(Yelling up the stairs.)* What are you doing? Let's GO!

OCEANA. *(Offstage.)* One second! *(Returning holding a coat and a large folded wool blanket.)* If we do manage to find her we can't bring her back here buck naked! What if we get pulled over? Or, stuck in a snow drift?

CORAL. Good thinking. Wait! *(She runs into the kitchen then from offstage.)* I thought of something else. *(She returns a moment later with a bowl of shrimp.)*

OCEANA. *(Eyeing the shrimp.)* You fixing to whip her up a shrimp cocktail?

CORAL. It may help us to lure her. In case she's wary of us.

> *(***CORAL*** *puts the bottle of Bacardi on the counter into her coat pocket.)*

OCEANA. She's not a stray dog, Coral. It's not like you can lure her with a piece of meat.

CORAL. I know that. But, she *is* like a porpoise. And, if she's been out of the water for any length of time she may get *hungry.*

OCEANA. And what's with the rum? You suppose she may get *thirsty* too?

CORAL. Don't be ridiculous. *I* may get thirsty. *(She takes the bottle out of her pocket, unscrews the cap and takes a swig from the bottle.)*

OCEANA. Give me that! *(She grabs the bottle of rum from* **CORAL** *and sets it back down on the counter.)*

CORAL. Hey! I may need a nip or two to keep warm.

OCEANA. We're not having a beach party!

CORAL. Anybody ever tell you you've become a real kill joy in your old age?

OCEANA. You do. Every day. You ready?

CORAL. I've been ready

OCEANA. Let's go.

> *(They exit via the offstage kitchen door carrying their wares and bickering, which fades out completely when the car door opens.)*

CORAL. I've been waiting on you.

OCEANA. Give me the keys.

CORAL. No way. I'm driving.

OCEANA. Forget it! You've been drinking. I'm driving!

CORAL. I had one nip. That hardly qualifies as drinking!

OCEANA. Tough. We're not getting pulled over on a DUI.

CORAL. Who's going to pull us over? Sheila's over at the bridge.

OCEANA. Give me the keys!

CORAL. *(Relenting.)* Fine! Here!

OCEANA. Thank you.

CORAL. If you're driving, why can't I drink?

OCEANA. Just get in the car.

> *(We hear car doors opening and closing and the car starting and pulling away. A moment or two later we catch a glimpse of **PEARL** through the window, cautiously stalking, like a cat, watching, listening. She is magnificently beautiful, soaking wet and completely naked [sheer body stocking] save for strategic patches of seaweed, sea grass, shells and jewelry consisting of an assortment of pearl and seashell necklaces, bracelets and earrings. **PEARL** is not in the least bothered by the cold. She has snowflakes in her long wet hair. **PEARL** has already almost completely transformed from mermaid to mortal and now has legs and feet which still sparkle with green, blue, purple, and turquoise flecks of glitter left over from her formerly spectacular mermaid fins. She also has a very cool pedicure with toenail polish that coordinates with her new legs. **PEARL** peeks in the cafe window. She*

then goes to the door, opens it, and enters leaving the door wide open behind her. Outside, the wind whips and and causes napkins and placemats to blow around inside the café. **PEARL** *explores the café, admiring salt, pepper and sugar shakers as if they were treasures and sniffs around. Her nose first leads her to the counter where she finds the open bottle of rum. She sniffs it a few times, takes a sip from the bottle, decides she likes it and takes a long drink after which she emits a satisfying burp which makes her giggle. Carrying the bottle, her she sniffs some more and her nose leads her into the kitchen. She returns carrying a handful of crabs and the rum bottle in the crook of her arm. She sits on the floor and contently begins to drink the rum and crack and eat the crabs, discarding cracked shells on the floor, as the lights fade to black.)*

(blackout)

Scene III

(*SETTING: The same. Hours later. It's almost dark.*)

(*AT RISE:* **PEARL** *is nowhere to be found, however, her presence is evidenced by the mess of crab shells littering the floor and the rum bottle, cap on, turned on its side on the floor. The front door to the café is still wide open and the wind has upended chairs and the café looks chaotic from the effects of both* **PEARL** *and the storm. Outside,* **FLOYD** *returns in his truck. We hear the engine turn off and the door shut.* **FLOYD** *enters to a semi-darkened café, carrying a sack of sand and a couple bags of salt.*)

FLOYD. (*Entering through the wide open front door, arms full and not watching where he's walking.*) Hello! Coral? Oceana? Anybody home? Got you some sal... WHOA!!!!!

(**FLOYD** *gives shriek as he slips on crab shells, trips over a overturned chair and falls flat on his back, dropping his bags and hitting his head on the floor. He's out cold – almost. Hearing the commotion,* **PEARL** *comes cautiously down from the upstairs apartment and sees* **FLOYD** *sprawled out in the middle of the floor. Curious, she approaches him, and begins to give him the once over, cautiously circling him and studying him from head to toe. She then kneels next to him and picks his arms, one by one, which drop to the floor as dead weight. She takes her finger and opens his eyelid one at a time. She puts her ear next to his mouth/nose to see if he is breathing. Satisfied that he is not dead,* **PEARL** *retrieves the rum bottle. She returns to him in a kneeling position and holds his head up with one arm against her glorious breasts [discretely covered with shells and jewelry] while holding the rum bottle to his lips with the other.* **FLOYD** *comes to for a brief moment.*)

FLOYD. *(Groggy, opening his eyes and trying to focus.)* What… what…what the hell is going on in here?

PEARL. *(Softly.)* Shhhhh.

FLOYD. Coral? *(He reaches up to to touch her face.)* Is that you?

PEARL. *(Softly cooing and feeding him the rum.)* Shhhhhh. *(She removes a pearl from her necklace and places it in the palm of his hand.)*

> **FLOYD,** *as if in a euphoric dream, looks in his palm at the pearl and realizes he is being cradled by a stunning half-naked angel/bartender/nursemaid feeding him rum shots. He takes it all with great appreciation and enthusiastically exclaims.)*

FLOYD. *(**Glory Hallelujah**!* **Praise be to God**! I've died and arrived at the Pearly Gates of Heaven!

> *(His head falls backwards on* **PEARL**'s *arm and he's once again unconscious. The sound of a car returning and car doors opening and closing is heard.* **PEARL**, *sensing potential danger, gently puts* **FLOYD**'s *head on the floor, and places the now empty rum bottle next to him. She scurries upstairs to hide as* **OCEANA** *and* **CORAL** *are heard offstage as they prepare to come in via the back door.)*

OCEANA. Well, she wasn't at the bridge.

CORAL. Good work, Sherlock. Glad you solved that one.

OCEANA. I knew she wouldn't be.

CORAL. You knew nothing of the sort.

OCEANA. Well, I do know one thing. I need a hot bath. I'm freezing.

CORAL. You're freezing? You weren't the one playing hide and seek in the Atlantic Ocean!

OCEANA. I warned you not to go in. But did you listen?? No! If you wind up with pneumonia you'll have no one to blame but yourself.

CORAL. Quit nagging me.

OCEANA. And take those silly things off your feet!

CORAL. If I could, I would! They have to thaw out first!

OCEANA. You ought to know by now, Coral. We don't have the constitution for frigid water like we did in the old days! When you get frostbite your toes *won't* grow back you know!

> *(As* **CORAL** *and* **OCEANA** *bicker in the kitchen offstage,* **MARINA** *enters the semi-dark café through the front door.)*

MARINA. You-hoo! Oceana! Coral! Where are you? Oh! *(She trips over* **FLOYD** *who is still out cold and sprawled on the floor. She shrieks and falls face down directly on top of* **FLOYD**'*s body.)* Owwwww! My ankle! Help! I sprained my ankle! Owwww. My ankle!

FLOYD. *(Awakened by the jolt and with* **MARINA**'*s fur coat covering him, screams.)* AAAAAAHHHH!

MARINA. *(In reply.)* AAAAAAHHHHH!

FLOYD. Get off of me! You Disciple of the Devil! You Hairy Beast! *(Frantically wrestling her off.)* Where is my Angel from heaven? What did you do with her? Help! Save me beautiful Angel! Save me from this hairy beast from hell!

MARINA. Let go of me! I'll have you arrested! Owwww! My ankle!

> *(Hearing the commotion in the café,* **OCEANA** *and* **CORAL** *[who wears scuba flippers and her winter coat, unbuttoned, over her bathing suit] run onstage from the kitchen.* **OCEANA** *turns on the lights to find* **MARINA** *sprawled out on top of* **FLOYD** *on the floor who is mightily trying to beat back the beast just as,* **NATHAN**, *a handsome, young, Coast Guard Lieutenant, off duty and not in uniform, enters the café from the wide open front door.)*

OCEANA. *(Seeing* **MARINA** *and* **FLOYD** *sprawled out on top of* **FLOYD**.*)* Marina! What in heaven's name are you doing to Floyd?

MARINA. He tripped me! I think my ankle is broken! Help me! *(***OCEANA** *helps her to a chair.)*

NATHAN. *(Politely knocking on open door.)* Excuse me.

CORAL. *(Harshly.)* **What** do *you* want?

NATHAN. Sorry to interrupt but the snow is coming down pretty hard out there and my rental car is stuck in a drift about a mile up the road. Is there any possibility I can get a room for the night and maybe a hot cup of coffee?

CORAL. *(Stomping clumsily to the front door in her flippers, she retrieves the closed sign, holds it with two hands above her head and proclaims to all of her uninvited guests.)* Can't anybody in this joint read English? We're **CLOSED**!

     *(**SHEILA** enters stomping the snow off her boots.)*

SHEILA. Not tonight you're not. Governor just declared a state of emergency. Everybody's got to stay off the roads till the plows come through tomorrow. *(Cheerfully.)* Looks like you Sea Hags got yourselves a house full of guests!

CORAL. Just my luck. Of all the friggin nights to have **No Vacancy**.

OCEANA. *(To **NATHAN**.)* Well then. Come on in. I guess we're *Open* after all. Have a seat. I'll put on a pot of fresh coffee.

NATHAN. Thank you, Ma'am. That's very kind of you.

OCEANA. And, I'll rustle us all up some chowder. Best on the island. *(She goes into the kitchen.)*

SHEILA. We all gotta stay put and hunker down right till the storm passes. Including me. *(She sees **FLOYD** on the floor.)* There you are, Floyd. Been trying to reach you to cover bridge duty tonight. No worries. I put flashing lights on a couple of saw horses. Nobody on the road anyway. Snow's too deep. I'll head back out at first light. Hey, whatcha doin layin on the floor?

CORAL. *(Picking up the empty Bacardi bottle.)* He's lapping up my liquor from the looks of it!

OCEANA. *(From kitchen.)* What happened to the crabs? They're all gone.

CORAL. *(Looking at mess on floor and then giving an evil eye to* **FLOYD** *as the culprit.)* They're shells all over the place. Looks like somebody's been having himself a king's feast in here. Huh, Floyd?

FLOYD. *(Getting up rubbing his head.)* The last thing I remember, I was delivering the salt. For your sidewalk.

CORAL. *(Seeing salt all over the floor.)* Last time I checked, *Pinky*, the sidewalk is *outside*. What's it doing all over the floor?

FLOYD. *(Recounting his actions.)* I came in. I slipped. I fell. I hit my head. I think. *(Remembering the best part.)* I DIED! And went to HEAVEN!

MARINA. *(Angrily taking off her boot an examining her ankle.)* If my ankle is broken you'll wish you stayed there when my lawyer gets through with you.

CORAL. Plug it, Toe Nail. *(to* **FLOYD**.*)* You *what?*

FLOYD. I DIED! I did! And, I got met at the Pearly Gates by a beautiful Angel. *(He remembers the* **PEARL** *she gave him.)* Look here! I can prove it. *(He holds out his hand and shows off the* **PEARL***)*. The Angel gave me a Pearl to welcome me to Heaven. *(As everyone is looking at the* **PEARL** *in* **FLOYD***'s hand,* **FLOYD** *glances up and sees* **PEARL** *who crept down the stairs and is peeking out behind the wall on the landing.)* And, there she is! *(Pointing.)* My Angel from Heaven! *(Everyone turns to look at* **PEARL** *standing on the staircase landing wrapped snugly in an colorful beach towel as the lights go quickly to black.)*

(blackout/curtain)

End of Act I

ACT II

Scene I

(SETTING: The same. A few moments later.)

(AT RISE: All eyes are on **PEARL**, *standing on the landing.)*

FLOYD. My Angel! You came back!

NATHAN. *(To* **PEARL***.)* It's you! *(He runs to her and takes her hand.)* I thought I never be able to find you. I was afraid I'd never see you again! *(He hugs her.)*

FLOYD. Hey! What do you think you're doing, pal. Get your hands off her. Find your own Angel.

OCEANA. *(To* **CORAL***.)* Uh oh. We're too late.

MARINA. Who is *she?* What's going on around here!

SHEILA. I'm not exactly sure. But whatever it is, it beats bridge duty.

FLOYD. *(Pulling* **NATHAN** *away.)* Didn't you hear me, buddy? Let go of my Angel!

NATHAN. With all due respect, mister. She's not you're Angel. She's my Mermaid! Now get your hands off me!

MARINA. Excuse me. Did you say that she is your *Mermaid?????*

NATHAN. I know how this sounds. But you have to believe me. *(To* **PEARL***.)* Tell them! Please! How you saved my life last night!

SHEILA. You mean you're the Coast Guard who went over the bridge last night? Why aren't you in the hospital?

FLOYD. I'm telling you one last time. Unhand my Angel or I'll...

NATHAN. You don't want to pick a fight with me, Pops. Unless you want to wind up on the floor again. Now back off. *(He shoves* **FLOYD** *away.)*

FLOYD. I'll show you who winds up on the floor. *(He grabs* **NATHAN**'s *jacket and is about to take a swing at him.)* Leave her alone! She's mine!

CORAL. *(Pulling him away.)* Pipe down, Pinky! That's enough! Listen to me. Both of you! *(To Pinky.)* She's not your *Angel. (To* **NATHAN**.) And, she's certainly not your *Mermaid! (Beat.)* She's *my* mermaid.

SHEILA. Since when do *you* have a mermaid?

CORAL. *(Taking* **PEARL**'s *hand and leading up back up the stairs.)* What's wrong with you people? When did a bunch of rationale adults start to believe in mermaids? Must be the snow storm! Makes everybody NUTS! This is *(She sees* **PEARL**'s *pearl necklace.)* ...Pearl. She's from The **MerMaids**. The cleaning service Oceana and I hired. Isn't that right, Oceana?

OCEANA. Yes! That's right! She… Pearl that is, just started. Today.

CORAL. *(Leading* **PEARL** *up the stairs offstage.)* Come along now, dear. Let's go get dressed. Can't you see? We have company!

SHEILA. She's from a cleaning service? *(Looking around at the mess, shaking her head.)* Doesn't look as if she made much progress.

OCEANA. *(Getting broom and starting to sweep.)* Give her a break. It's her first day on the job.

MARINA. *(To* **OCEANA**.) I don't see how you can afford to hire a live in housekeeper when you can't even meet your financial obligations to the bank. I'll be sure to tell *the Captain* about this.

NATHAN. *(Despondent, to* **FLOYD**.) Look, mister. I'm sorry. I don't usually act this way. I feel like a real jerk. But, it all seemed so real. I guess I was hallucinating after all. They told me at the hospital that it's pretty common. Hallucinations from hypothermia, that is. That ocean *is* pretty cold. *(He puts his hand out to shake* **FLOYD**'s.*)* Name's Nathan Crowley. Pleased to meet you. And, I hope you'll accept my apology.

FLOYD. *(Shaking* **NATHAN**'s *hand.)* Floyd Ferguson. Happy to oblige, Nathan. No harm done. And, I know firsthand how cold that ocean is. I took a dunk once myself this time of year. Years ago. Wound up in the hospital with a bout of pneumonia. Recall having a hallucination or two myself. *(Patting him on the back and leading him to a table where the both sit.)* No harm done. And, if it's any consolation, I thought that housekeeper gal was an Angel. Guess I knocked my noggin harder than I thought when I took a spill on the floor. *(To* **OCEANA**.*)* Didn't know about your new chamber maid. Didn't see her this morning.

OCEANA. She hadn't arrived yet. Got here after you left this morning.

SHEILA. *(Looking around at the mess.)* Well, I hope she did a better job upstairs than she did down here. Otherwise I'd have a bone to pick with that cleaning service if I were you.

OCEANA. Listen everybody. I'm going to put on a pot of chowder. It'll have to be vegetarian because we seem to be out of crabs. Since you're all stuck here for the night, why don't you all pick out a room upstairs and settle in. I'll bring you up some food when it's ready. Each guest room has a double bed, a TV and radio. So you'll all be pretty comfortable unless the power goes out.

NATHAN. Thank you, ma'am. I apologize for my behavior.

OCEANA. Apology accepted. You've been though a lot. I'm glad you're all right. Now, go on up and get settled. *(Chasing everyone up the stairs.)* Go on, claim your rooms. I'll be up in an hour or so with your supper.

MARINA. And just how do you expect me to climb those stairs with this ankle?

OCEANA. You stay here. I need help in the kitchen.

MARINA. I don't cook!

OCEANA. You will tonight.

MARINA. That's what servants are for! Why can't the new girl help you?

SHEILA. I'll help you, Oceana.

OCEANA. No. Thanks anyway, Sheila. You go on up. I have some business to discuss with Marina. *(She goes into the kitchen and leaves* **MARINA** *sitting at the table.)*

SHEILA. All right, then. But if you change your mind let me know. *(She follows the others upstairs.* **OCEANA** *goes into the kitchen and returns with an armful of potatoes and peeler.)*

OCEANA. *(From kitchen.)* Thanks. I will. *(She returns with a bowl full of potatoes and two peeling knives.)*

MARINA. I hope you don't expect me to peel potatoes!

OCEANA. *(Handing* **MARINA** *a knife.)* Oh, go whine to *the Captain.* By the way, what are you doing here? Where is the Captain? *(***OCEANA** *begins to peel potatoes.)*

MARINA. *The Captain* was detained in the city. I returned in a taxi. But the sissy cab driver wouldn't take me all the way home due to the roads. *(She cries.)* Oh, Oceana!

OCEANA. Marina, what's wrong?

MARINA. Everything!

OCEANA. What do you mean?

MARINA. It's *the Captain!*

OCEANA. What about the Captain?

MARINA. He left me!

OCEANA. Left you?

MARINA. Yes!

OCEANA. Where?

MARINA. In *the city!*

OCEANA. I don't follow.

MARINA. Do I have to spell it out for you? It's *over* between *the Captain* and me! Over! Done! Finished! Kaput!

OCEANA. I had no idea that you two were having problems.

MARINA. He's been impossible. Ever since my treasure ran out.

OCEANA. It did? When?

MARINA. Two months ago. I didn't expect it to last forever. Not the way *the Captain* blows through money. Yachts and luxury cars don't grow on trees, you know. I'm surprised, quite frankly, that my treasure lasted as long as it did.

OCEANA. I had no idea.

MARINA. *The Captain* lured me into the city today to his lawyer's office. I thought we were in for a fun day. Foreclosing on properties. Having lunch at The Bellevue to celebrate. You know. That kind of thing. Like we usually do. But when we got to his lawyer's office *the Captain* served me with dissolution papers! Told me that I was of no further use to him! Of course, I was forced to sign then and there. He kicked me to the curb like an empty can of salmon. And, the real kicker is, all of our assets are in *the Captain's* name! *(She wails.)* Oh, Oceana, I'm such a fool! *(Beat.) You* know how that is!

OCEANA. Unfortunately, I do. Thanks for reminding me.

MARINA. *(Blowing her nose with a handkerchief.)* You're welcome.

OCEANA. Marina, I don't understand. Why would you sign papers? You need your own lawyer. To represent your interests. There are community property laws. Surely you are entitled to half the marital assets. You'll make out okay even if the Captain was a big spender.

MARINA. Marital assets? Ha! *The Captain* and I are not *legally* married! You can't *legally* marry a mermaid, Oceana! The documents were *dissolution* papers not divorce papers. To dissolve our partnership. And, if I try to pursue my common law rights, *the Captain* threatened to expose me for what I really am. A mermaid! Can you just imagine? They'll lock me away in a Maritime Museum. Stick me with pins and needles day after day.

Poke and prod me every which way. *(Beat.)* Which *might* be fun…for a while. But then they'll probably try to drown me in a shark tank to see how long I can hold my breath under water. And after all this time, although I did quit smoking *years ago*, is probably no more than thirty minutes. At best!

OCEANA. Well, that's quite a story. I don't know quite what to say. *(She rises and goes behind the counter and gets a bottle of whisky and two glasses and puts them on the table.)* But, maybe this will help. If only temporarily. *(She pours two glasses.)*

MARINA. *(Dabbing her eyes with a handkerchief.)* It would help even more with a chaser. *(She tosses back the whisky straight up.)*

OCEANA. *(Going into the kitchen to get the beer.)* I'll be right back.

> *(*CORAL *and* PEARL *come down from upstairs. Both are dressed in jeans, sweaters and shoes or sneakers.* CORAL *sees* MARINA *helping herself to a second shot of whisky.)*

CORAL. Drink up, *Toe Nail.* Each shot you knock back is going on your tab. Oh! Did I mention we raised the room rates today? You get the special "friends and family rate" of fifteen hundred a night. Course I did save our best room for you. Two drafty windows instead of one. After all, what are kissing cousins for?

MARINA. That's a wonderful idea, Coral. Please be sure to send the bill to *the Captain.* I couldn't care less what you overcharge the conniving scoundrel. In fact, why don't you charge *three thousand* a night. Surely you could command that much, especially for a suite with an ocean view and *(She holds up her glass.)* inflated mini-bar prices.

> *(*OCEANA *enters with a six pack of beer.)*

CORAL. What did you put in her whisky? She's not her usual revolting self.

OCEANA. The Captain dumped her. Marina is just as broke as we are. Her treasure finally ran out.

CORAL. *(Stunned, then excited.)* No shit!

MARINA. Au contraire, Coral. *The Captain **is** a piece of…*

CORAL. *(Elated, dancing around laughing.)* Ha! Ha! *(She grabs **OCEANA** and swings her around.)* Ha! Ha! Ha! You know what this means, don't you? Ha! Marina wasn't the smart one after all! She's just as stupid as we were! More so even! *(To **MARINA**.)* With age doesn't come wisdom after all! You had years of opportunity to run off with the rest of your treasure and you blew it! On *the Captain!* That makes you the biggest ninny of us all.

MARINA. *(Referring to **PEARL**.)* I really wish you wouldn't defame me in front of the hired help, Coral. It's uncouth.

CORAL. *(Checking up the stairs to make sure nobody is looking or listening.)* Since you are now an official member of our Miserable Middle Age Mermaid's Club – Hell, Toe Nail, you're our newly elected President – I'll let you in on a little secret. *(Putting arm around **PEARL**.)* Pearl here isn't really the hired help.

MARINA. No? Then who is she?

OCEANA. Glad you're sitting down. Pearl is…one of *us.*

MARINA. *(Enviously eyeing **PEARL**.)* She doesn't look middle age and miserable.

CORAL. You're not only broke, Marina. You're dumb as a stump.

MARINA. *(Crying.)* I know. I know.

CORAL. Listen to me. Pearl is a mermaid.

MARINA. You said. From the cleaning service.

OCEANA. Marina! Pearl is *(Imitates swimming.)* a mermaid. Like we used to be!

MARINA. *(Gasps.)* I knew it! I sensed something… indescribable…yet vaguely familiar…when I awoke this morning. I felt her presence in the vicinity. That's what I wanted to talk to you about this morning…to ask if you sensed it too…but the Captain was having a royal hissy fit in the limo. Yelling at the driver to blow his horn to hurry me up. To think that when I rescued him from that shipwreck all those years ago he was a nothing but a lowly deck hand. He'd still be swabbing poop decks if it weren't for me. The only reason he's even a *Captain* is because my treasure bought him that ninety-foot yacht. I may be broke, Ana, but I honestly don't miss that arrogant blowfish.

CORAL. Takes one to know one, Toe Nail.

MARINA. I wouldn't be so smug if I were you. Before *the Captain* served me with papers today, he began foreclosure proceedings on *your* establishment. You probably won't believe me, but I did try to stop him. We are cousins, after all. Although you can't say I haven't warned you about paying up.

CORAL. Can't pay what you don't have. And, may I remind you, *cousin*, we didn't approach the Captain for a loan in the first place. You two came to us. Insisted that if we borrowed money from your bank we could make some needed renovations around here and triple our seasonal income.

OCEANA. That's right, Marina. We were very upfront with the Captain as to our hesitation about loan repayments in the off season. We wanted to wait it out. I admit we share a burden of responsibility but he did rather pressure us to sign the papers.

MARINA. Of course he did. How else do you think he came to own half the island. Using my treasure and foreclosing on suckers like the two of you!

CORAL. Hey now!

OCEANA. Okay, let's calm down. We'll work something out.

CORAL. How?

OCEANA. I don't know. Somehow. In the meantime, we have to talk some sense into Pearl.

MARINA. How can we possibly talk sense into Pearl when we haven't got any ourselves?

CORAL. I hate to admit it, but she has a point.

OCEANA. Because we have *experience.*

MARINA. I don't even know what you're talking about. *(Eyeing* **PEARL***.)* And why does she just stand there? Stone silent. Looking fabulous. In those jeans. Like I used to. And, if I say so myself, still do. *(She tosses her hair like a model.)* I haven't heard her utter a single syllable since I arrived. What's wrong, honey? Catfish got your tongue?

OCEANA. Have you forgotten, Marina? Pearl can't speak yet. Her voice box won't mature until she's out of the water for at least twenty four hours.

CORAL. Yeah, if she tries to speak now she'll shatter all the windows within a mile radius and all the dogs on the island will begin to howl.

MARINA. Oh, that's right. I made that mistake myself when I first swam ashore. I was in the backseat of a car with *the Captain.* We were…well…you know…in the midst of "resuscitation activities." I whispered in the Captain's ear and blew the rear car window clear across town. And, the dogs did go crazy. Especially *the Captain.*

OCEANA. Too much information!

MARINA. Anyway, what kind of infinite wisdom are three of us supposed to bestow on young Pearl? She seems to be doing just fine on her own. *(To* **PEARL***.)* By the way, what size are those jeans? *(Holds her hand up.)* I forgot. You can't talk yet. *(Shaking her head realizing that she'd never fit into them.)* It's probably for the better. *(She gestures for* **PEARL** *to sit down.)* Take a seat, honey. Have a potato. Load up on some carbs. It'll do you good.

> *(***PEARL*** sits and ***MARINA*** tosses her a potato and hands her the knife which ***OCEANA*** grabs before ***PEARL*** can harm herself with it. She shoots ***MARINA*** a dirty look and hands her back the knife and another potato.)*

OCEANA. You're still on K.P.

MARINA. Okay. Okay.

CORAL. Oceana and I spent all day at the beach. Looking for Pearl.

MARINA. You knew she was coming?

OCEANA. No. Sheila told us about the bridge accident and that Nathan told a rescuer that he'd been saved by a mermaid.

MARINA. Who is Nathan?

OCEANA. The young man upstairs. Pearl rescued him late last night. When his car went off the Seaspray Bridge.

MARINA. Is he a sailor?

OCEANA. Coast Guard. He came back to find her.

MARINA. Of course he did. They always come back.

CORAL. *(To* **OCEANA.***)* See! Even *she* knows they always come back.

MARINA. So, we're supposed to…what? Warn her about the perils and pitfalls of falling in love with mortal men? So she doesn't wind up heartbroken and penniless, like us?

CORAL. Exactly!

MARINA. I see. *(Thinks.)* Well, why don't you just turn on the television and let her watch a couple reruns of *Sex and the City.* That ought to do it.

CORAL. *(To* **OCEANA,** *referring to* **MARINA.***)* I'll be damned. Toe Nail is smarter than us after all.

MARINA. *(to* **PEARL.***)* Listen, sweetie. CAN – YOU – UN-DER-STAND – WHAT – I'M – SAY-ING?

> (**PEARL** *nods affirmatively.*)

Good. Take our advice. GO – BACK – TO – THE – SEA. Your young sailor upstairs isn't worth it.

> (**PEARL** *shakes her head in disagreement.*)

Now! You listen. We know! We've been where you are. Have you been listening to my tale of woe?

> (**PEARL** *nods her head.*)

I was involved with *the Captain* for nearly thirty years! Thirty years! In the beginning, I was sure that **love would**

keep us together. *(She realizes what she just said, cringes and shoots a look to* **CORAL***) **Don't say it!***

CORAL. *(Smirking.)* I'm just listening. *(Beat.)* **Toe Nail.**

MARINA. *(Continuing to* **PEARL***.)* But, when my treasure finally ran out, *the Captain* discarded me like a worn out life ring! I know I was supposed to relinquish my treasure all at once in consideration of my falling in love with a human. I admit it. *I broke the rules.* But, I did it as more or less a marine insurance policy. To keep *the Captain* around. After all, I saw how things turned out for Coral and Oceana and I didn't' want to end up like them. My scheme actually worked for quite a long while. I safeguarded my treasure. *The Captain* never knew where. But, it ran out eventually. And, with the way the price of gold fluctuates these days on the open market, your treasure may not even be worth as much as you think! Oh sure, you're young and beautiful and rich *now.* But, when your beauty starts to fade, and age creeps up on you like a hungry cockroach, and your sailor spends your treasure on silly boy toys, you'll curse the day you shimmied out of the ocean. So, shoo! Go back! Before it's too late. *The clock is ticking!*

> **(PEARL** *pouts, crosses her arms in front of her and emphatically shakes her head, No!)*

CORAL. Yes, Pearl! Marina is right. Please go! Jump off a bridge and high tail it out of here! Before you find out the hard way that Nathan has a wife and four kids stashed away in Venezuela!

> **(PEARL** *emphatically shakes her head, No!)*

OCEANA. Swim fast, Pearl! So you never have to learn the truth that your manly and macho sailor boy, Nathan, has a *boyfriend* or two waiting for him in *Norway!*

> **(PEARL** *looks grief stricken and loudly gasps with horror.)*

MARINA. *(Dryly, to* **OCEANA***.)* I think you just had a breakthrough.

OCEANA. That's right, Pearl! My sailor, Hans, turned out to be *gay*. Ah, NOT "happy" gay. "Gay" gay! Do you know what "gay" means? I'll tell you what "gay" means! "Gay" means that your sailor, *Nathan*, may have a boyfriend named *Juergen* in Oslo, and the two of *them* will live happily ever after spending *your* treasure on all types of *gay* Norwegian things, that they'll probably buy from *Ikea*, which make the two of them very *happy*!

> (**PEARL***'s face crumbles and she begins to cry loudly. The windows rattle, pictures fall from the walls.*)

MARINA. There, there. It'll be all right. Let's get you out of here. Back to the sea. Where you belong. All right?

> (**PEARL**, *heartbroken, relents and nods her head, yes.*)

Oh, drat. I'd love to watch you swim off. But, I just realized with the roads the way they are, you're going to have to walk. It's only a few blocks but I can't very well go with you with my ankle the way it is.

OCEANA. That's all right, Marina. Coral and I will manage. You've been a great help. Thank you.

CORAL. Toe Nail, I give credit where it's due. We couldn't have convinced her without your help.

MARINA. It's about time you recognized my potential. (*To* **PEARL**.) Well, so long dearie. Nice meeting you. I'm going to attempt to hobble upstairs now for a siesta. (*She hops and hobbles to the stairs and turns back to* **PEARL**.) Oh, and when you get home, if anyone from the old neighborhood asks how we're doing, be sure to tell them…*we're just fine*. (*She winks and exits.*)

> (*blackout/curtain*)

Scene II

(SETTING: The same. Later that evening.)

(AT RISE: The café is dark. **FLOYD** *enters from the upstairs and turns on the lights.)*

FLOYD. *(Looking around.)* Coral? Oceana? Supper ready yet? I'm getting kinda hungry.

> *(***FLOYD*** *exits to the kitchen and returns a moment later carrying a bowl of chowder and a spoon and sets it on the table which has the bottle of whiskey. He gets a glass for the whisky and dish of oyster crackers from the counter, sits down at the table, pours himself a shot, crumbles some oyster crackers in his bown and begins to eat.* **NATHAN** *comes down from upstairs and sees* **FLOYD** *eating.)*

NATHAN. Mind if I join you?

FLOYD. Help yourself. Crock pot's in the kitchen. Seems to be self-serve.

NATHAN. Awesome. I'm starved.

> *(***NATHAN*** *exits to the kitchen.* **FLOYD** *gets up, goes behind the counter to get* **NATHAN** *a glass for whiskey and sets it down on the table.* **NATHAN** *returns a moment later carrying a bowl of chowder and a spoon.)*

FLOYD. Pour you a shot?

NATHAN. Thank you. *(Crumbling oyster crackers in his bowl.)* Don't mind if I do. *(***NATHAN*** *begins to eat and as he does he makes a grunting sound and shakes his head.)*

FLOYD. What's wrong? Don't like the grub? It'd be better with some blue points in it.

NATHAN. *(Deep in thought.)* Huh? Oh. No. I was just thinking. I'm going to be the laughing stock when I get back to the base. I'll never live this one down. Seeing a mermaid. Of all things! *(He takes a drink of whiskey.)*

FLOYD. You were alone, weren't you? If you don't spill the beans, how will your buddies know?

NATHAN. My Commanding Officer came to the hospital this morning. The doctor had to give him a full report. For my file. Told them I'm fine, considering the accident, but that I had been hallucinating. Insisted that a mermaid saved me. Now I'm on medical leave for a couple of days. I dread the thought of going back. The guys will crucify me.

FLOYD. Your C.O. a blabbermouth?

NATHAN. The worst kind. When I get back the guys will probably have a big plastic blow up mermaid doll on my bunk with a big sign tied to her with some raunchy saying. I'll be the butt of all mermaid jokes for years to come.

FLOYD. Boys will be boys. You'd probably do the same.

NATHAN. I've probably done worse. Now I'll be the one on the receiving end.

FLOYD. What comes around goes around.

NATHAN. You can say that again. *(Agitated, he gets up and walks around.)* I never knew that hallucinations could be so real. That's why I came back, I guess. To try to find her. The mermaid. To prove that she wasn't just my imagination. And that's not even the craziest thing!

FLOYD. No?

NATHAN. No! I know this sounds corny but, do you believe in love at first sight? I actually fell in love with her! Head over heels! Crazy, madly in love! With a mermaid! She was so beautiful, and loving, and caring! I know this sounds cliché but I felt like I knew her. Like we were meant to be together. Forever. No one has ever had that effect on me before. I'm not the impulsive type. I've never even been in love. Until now. I'm absolutely miserable. She *is* real. I know she is. And, I have to find her!

FLOYD. *(Shakes his head, he's been there and knows what it's like.)* Sit down. *(Pouring them both another shot of whiskey.)* I'll let you in on a little secret. But you have to promise to keep it to yourself.

NATHAN. *(Sits, despondent.)* What's that?

FLOYD. Mums the word?

NATHAN. *(Shrugs.)* Sure.

FLOYD. You're not the only one around here who fell in love with a mermaid.

NATHAN. What? Who?

> **(FLOYD** *nods his head.)*

You?

FLOYD. Yup.

NATHAN. Nah. You're just saying that. To make me feel better.

FLOYD. Nope. It's true.

NATHAN. When?

FLOYD. About thirty years ago. I was working on a boat. Mile or two off shore. It was night time. I was up on deck staring up at the sky, contemplating the dark side of the moon, when all of a sudden this gigantic tidal wave hit. Outta the blue. Boat turned over and I fell into the big drink along with every body else. I was underwater trying to figure out which way was up when I saw a magnificent glowing light. Then another! Then another! I saw *three* mermaids that day!

NATHAN. Are you for real or are you just spinning an old sailor's yarn?

FLOYD. Keep interrupting me and I won't tell the rest.

NATHAN. Sorry. Go on.

FLOYD. I came to the surface and saw the first mermaid unhitch a lifeboat and load in women and children. And she pushed them toward shore.

NATHAN. There were women and children on the boat?

FLOYD. A few. It was a multi-purpose vessel.

NATHAN. Then what happened?

FLOYD. I'm treading water and I see the first mermaid come back and go on to rescue the ship's interior decorator.

NATHAN. The ship had an *interior decorator*???

FLOYD. Yup. Scandinavian fellow as I recall. All kinds of jobs on a ship. The Captain was redoing his quarters. I sneaked a peek at the sketches. Would have been very plush if the ship didn't sink.

NATHAN. What about the other two mermaids? What where they doing?

FLOYD. The second mermaid righted the ship and loaded some men into another lifeboat and shoved it toward the shore. Then I saw her scoop up Poopy.

NATHAN. *Poopy*???

FLOYD. Poopy was his nickname. He was the deck hand who swabbed the poop deck. Forget his real name. Didn't really know him that well.

NATHAN. What about the third mermaid?

FLOYD. She loaded up another lifeboat and gave it a huge push toward land. Then, she swam over to rescue me. She was the most beautiful sight I ever saw. I fell in love. Instantly. Just like you did.

NATHAN. You did? What happened?

FLOYD. I had to let her go. Or, I should say, I had to make her let me go.

NATHAN. Why?

FLOYD. You see, I could swim. I was getting mighty tired but still holding my own. Treading water. The mermaid scooped me up and started off to the shore with me. Then, I saw my buddy in the water. He wasn't a good swimmer. Not like me. He was drowning. Going under for the third time. And, that water was cold!

(**NATHAN** *nods in agreement.*)

I knew my pal had a wife and four kids back home so I pleaded with the mermaid to save him instead.

NATHAN. So she did? You didn't drown?

FLOYD. No. The mermaid took care of me too. Latched me on to a piece of driftwood. Gave me a good shove toward the shore. I made it too. Few hours later. But before she shoved me off, she put this in my pocket. To remember her by. As if I could ever forget her. *(He reaches in to his pocket and pulls out a gold and emerald pendant and shows it to* **NATHAN**.*)*

NATHAN. *(Admiring the pendant, whistling.)* That's something. Surely one of a kind. You think it's real?

FLOYD. Don't know. Don't care. Never tried to sell it. Been carrying it round with me for the better part of thirty years. *(He takes it back and puts in his pocket but misses and it falls to the floor under the table.* **FLOYD** *is too tipsy to notice.)*

NATHAN. What happened to your mermaid? Ever see her again?

FLOYD. No. And believe me, I looked. And looked. And looked some more. Searched for her for years. Up and down the coast. I was completely smitten. Miserable in love. I would have traded all the tea in China, given all the money I had, which wasn't much at the time, but still a tidy sum, to see her just once again.

NATHAN. And your friend, with the wife and kids, he lived?

FLOYD. Fernando. Yup. He lived. Never saw him again after that though. Heard through the grapevine that he struck it rich somehow. Found himself a buried treasure somewhere. And took it all home to Venezuela to his wife and kids.

NATHAN. What a story!

FLOYD. Yup.

NATHAN. You swear it's true.

FLOYD. Yup. I'm not the sort who could make something like that up.

NATHAN. So, are you still looking for her, your mermaid? After thirty years?

FLOYD. Well, yes and no. Eventually I came to the conclusion that life goes on. Years later I was blessed to meet a fine woman and I was able to persuade her to be my wife. We were very happy for fifteen years. Bought a home. Traveled around. Life was good. Then, things took a turn and my wife became ill. She passed a couple years ago.

NATHAN. I'm sorry.

FLOYD. So am I.

NATHAN. You still think about her? I mean, the mermaid?

FLOYD. I think about Marilyn, my wife. And the mermaid. Every single day. Guess I will for the rest of my life. (*He gets up from table and takes his bowl/spoon to the kitchen.*) Well, I'm about ready to call it a night. (*He returns and exits up to bed leaving* **NATHAN** *sitting at the table.*) Good night.

NATHAN. Good night, Floyd. Thanks for confiding in me. I feel a lot better. And, don't worry. Your secret is safe with me.

FLOYD. (*Offstage.*) Yup.

> (**NATHAN** *sits for a moment in deep thought about the story that* **FLOYD** *has just told him and knocks back another shot of whisky. A moment or two later,* **PEARL** *peeps in the window, sees* **NATHAN** *and knocks.* **NATHAN** *sees her, runs to the door and lets her in. She has wet hair and is wearing the sheer mermaid body stocking with jewelry and shells, etc. as in Act 1.* **PEARL** *jumps into* **NATHAN**'s *arms and they share a long kiss.*)

NATHAN. It *is* you, isn't it?

> (**PEARL** *nods her head yes and kisses him again.*)

You're not the housekeeper are you?

> (**PEARL** *shakes her head 'no.'*)

I'm not crazy! I wasn't hallucinating after all was I?

> (**PEARL** *shakes her head no and kisses him again.*)

(Realizes he's been drinking quite a bit, picks up the whiskey bottle.) Oh no. I'm not passed out am I?

(PEARL *shakes her head no and kisses him again.)*

NATHAN. Good. *(He starts to blather.)* Because I love you! I do! I love you! From the moment I saw you! Now, I know you don't even know me but I assure you, I'm not crazy. I don't say that to everybody. I've never told another girl I love her. I'm not a weirdo or a criminal or a stalker or a…

(PEARL *kisses him again and leads him to the stairs. He picks her up and carries her.)*

Do you love me too? Now, you don't have to answer me yet. Just think about it.

(PEARL *grabs his neck and kisses him once more as they exit upstairs.)*

(A moment or two later, **CORAL** *and* **OCEANA** *return.)*

CORAL. Well, we did it. She swam away.

OCEANA. *(Sadly.)* Yes, she did.

CORAL. She'll live happy ever after with some slippery male merman in the deep blue sea. Where she belongs.

OCEANA. Yes, she will.

CORAL. What's wrong? We have a happy ending?

OCEANA. Do we?

CORAL. I thought so.

OCEANA. Hmmmm.

CORAL. What's the matter?

OCEANA. I'm having second thoughts. I don't know if we did the right thing.

CORAL. Meaning?

OCEANA. What if her sailor, Nathan, *doesn't* have a wife and four kids? What if he *doesn't* have a boyfriend tucked away in Oslo? What if he's *not* just after her treasure? What if…he really *loves* her?

CORAL. *(Shaking her head.)* You've gotta return those DVDs.

OCEANA. *(Grabs* CORAL*'s arm, loudly.)* What if we're *WRONG?*

SHEILA. *(Yelling from the upstairs,* CORAL *and* OCEANA *are startled and look up the staircase.)* **Hey! Hold it right there! Where do you two think you're going? *Come back!*** *(Beat.)* I mean it! ***Stop*****!!!!** You can't leave yet. We're still in a state of emergency! I'll write you both up!

> **(SHEILA** *comes running down from upstairs and goes to the door, opens it and runs out.)*

COME BACK HERE OR YOU'RE UNDER ARREST!

> *(She returns a moment later.)*

You were *wrong,* all right.

CORAL. Huh? About what?

SHEILA. *(Coming back in.)* Your new housekeeper? Well, she's history! I hope she didn't run off with anything valuable.

OCEANA. What are you talking about?

SHEILA. You know, sometimes they work in pairs. I was a bit suspicious of that young fellow too. Bet his rental car isn't really stuck in a drift. Probably has a big truck parked in the next block and they used it as a getaway vehicle. Happens all the time. Trust me, you'll never see that girl again. I'd take a thorough inventory and then call that cleaning service first thing in the morning to report her if I were you.

CORAL. You mean Pearl? She…she…left. Suddenly.

SHEILA. She sure did. Like a thief in the night.

OCEANA. What?

SHEILA. I fell asleep. Then my stomach started grumbling and woke me up. By the way, did I miss supper?

OCEANA. Supper! It's in the crock pot. I'm sure it's ready.

CORAL. Hold on. You saw Pearl? When?

SHEILA. She and that boyfriend of hers. I woke up and went into the bathroom. Looked outside and saw them climbing out his window. Climbed down the fire escape to the back deck and ran off together. I yelled at them but they didn't stop. They just ran off, holding hands, in the snow. Laughing and kissing. Then, they stopped, turned around, waved at me and ran off.

CORAL. I don't believe it. Pearl came back. After all.

SHEILA. Haven't you been listening? She's *gone*. She took off.

(**FLOYD** *comes down stairs.*)

FLOYD. What's all the racket?

SHEILA. That young man and the housekeeper. They took off together.

FLOYD. They did? So! He found her after all. Well, good for them.

SHEILA. I'm so angry! Two thieves right here under this roof. On my watch no less. I'm so sorry Oceana. I should have followed my instincts about those two. I'd venture to guess they nabbed all your fine jewelry.

OCEANA. Ha! Don't worry, Sheila. We don't have any.

SHEILA. *(Sees the pendant that* **FLOYD** *dropped on the floor.)* No? Well then what's this? They probably dropped it while they were looting the kitchen for silver.

(**CORAL** *recognizes the pendant and gasps.*)

CORAL. My pendant! *(She snatches the pendant from* **SHEILA.***)* Where did this come from?

FLOYD. *(Snatching the pendant from* **CORAL.***)* Hold on now. That's *my* pendant! I showed it to Nathan. Never showed it to anyone before tonight. It must have fallen out of my pocket.

CORAL. *Your* pendant?

FLOYD. That's right.

CORAL. I don't believe you. Where did you get it?

FLOYD. None of your business.

CORAL. I want to know!

FLOYD. Had it a long time.

CORAL. That's not what I asked. Where did you get it?

FLOYD. It was a gift.

CORAL. A gift? From whom?

FLOYD. An old friend. You wouldn't understand.

CORAL. No! That's *my* pendant. It's one of a kind. It's engraved on the back. Two hearts intertwined with an anchor.

FLOYD. How did *you* know that?

CORAL. I told you it's mine! That is, it used to be mine. *(She thinks.)* I gave it to… I gave it to… *(She looks at **FLOYD** as if for the first time in years.)*…to **you**?

FLOYD. *(Catching on to the unbelievable coincidence.)* You mean, **she**…was **you**? You're **her**???

CORAL. You mean… I gave my pendant to… *(Grimacing.)* **YOU**????

FLOYD. *(Giving **CORAL** the once over.)* No way. NO WAY!!! **You're**…**her**???

CORAL. This is incredible. Are you telling me…you mean… you're **him**?

CORAL & FLOYD. *(They study each other for a beat, simultaneously turn away from each other and shake their head. Then, together they exclaim.)* **NAAAAAAAHHHHHH!!!!!!!!.**

FLOYD. *(Coming to grips that it may be possible after all.)* That was **really**…you?

CORAL. 'Fraid so. **She** was **me**. And, **he**…was **you**. *(Shaking her head.)* I can't believe it.

FLOYD. *(In disbelief and with sincerity.)* I searched for you. For years.

CORAL. *(Taken back.)* You did?

FLOYD. Yes. For years. I kind of hoped you would have come back for me.

CORAL. *(Referring to her rotten luck with Fernando.)* Believe me, I wish I had.

FLOYD. When you didn't, I started looking for you. Everywhere.

CORAL. Well. *(Beat.)* I guess you finally found me.

FLOYD. *(He scratches his head.)* After all these years. *(Smiling.)* I finally did, didn't I?

CORAL. *(Referring to the fact that she doesn't quite look like the deep sea diva she did 30 years ago.)* Hope you're not too disappointed.

FLOYD. Disappointed? Never! *(He reaches for her hand.)*

CORAL. Really?

FLOYD. After all these years, I can finally say, *you* are worth every second of the wait. *(They lock eyes and **FLOYD** takes **CORAL**'s hand, pulls her toward him, and gives her a "I've been waiting for 30 long years to get to do this" type of kiss.)*

(Handing her the pendant.) Do you want it back?

CORAL. No. It served its purpose. You keep it. *(They kiss again, this time a little shorter.)*

OCEANA. *(Dabbing her eyes with a paper napkin.)* So there Coral! There are such things as happy endings, huh! You should start watching my DVDs.

CORAL. *(To **FLOYD**, returning to her old cranky self.)* Hold on a minute. I thought you couldn't stand me.

FLOYD. That's odd. I thought *you* couldn't stand *me.*

CORAL. I couldn't stand *you* because I thought you couldn't stand *me!*

FLOYD. If I couldn't stand you, why would I come here for breakfast every morning and drink your lousy coffee?

CORAL. *(Pretending to be offended.)* Watch it now!

(They smile and kiss again – after all, they're making up for 30 years of lost time.)

SHEILA. Well, I have no idea what's happening around here, but to be honest, I'm too hungry to care.

OCEANA. Oh! Follow me. I'll get you a big bowl of...

(Horn blows from outside.)

SHEILA. Well, what do you know! There's Larry. Come to get me in the Hummer. *(She goes to the door and shouts outside.)* You shouldn't be driving, hon. I'll have to put the cuffs on you when we get home! *(She chuckles.)* Yeah,

I know you like it when I do that. Hold on. I'll be out in a minute!

CORAL. I'll get your things! *(She runs upstairs.)*

OCEANA. I'll pack up some chowder "to go" for you and Larry. *(She runs into the kitchen.)*

SHEILA. *(To* **FLOYD***.)* So, I take it you and Coral are *an item?*

FLOYD. Yup.

SHEILA. Pretty funny for two people who hated each other's guts this morning.

FLOYD. Yup.

SHEILA. Well, I guess stranger things have happened. Love can be a strange and beautiful twist of fate.

FLOYD. Yup.

> *(***CORAL** *returns with* **SHEILA***'s coat, hat and scarf. As* **SHEILA** *gets dressed for the weather she shouts out the door.)*

SHEILA. I'll be right there, Lar. Ana's getting us some soup to go. Oh, look! Larry's got the new mutt in the back. *(To* **FLOYD** *and* **CORAL***.)* You two love birds wouldn't be interested in starting a family right away would you? I know a real sweet Golden Retriever out there who'd be interested in adoption.

FLOYD. *(Putting his arm around* **CORAL***.)* Up to you? What do you think? *Mother?*

CORAL. I did always want a baby to spoil.

FLOYD. Marilyn and I weren't blessed with children. I'd kind of like to be a father myself. Although at my age I'd be more of a grandfather.

CORAL. Works for me! *(To* **SHEILA***.)* We'll take him! Er, is he a "he" or a "she"

SHEILA. A he.

CORAL. *(To* **FLOYD***.)* What should we name him?

FLOYD. *(Thinks for a minute.)* How 'bout Nathan?

CORAL. Perfect!

FLOYD. I'll go get him. *(***FLOYD** *runs out to retrieve* **NATHAN***, the Golden Retriever.)*

CORAL. *(Shouting out the door.)* Bring Nathan around the back. We can feed him in the kitchen.

SHEILA. Well…you know, I'm also the L&I inspector on this island. No doggies allowed in kitchens unless they're service dogs. But, I'll look the other way. Just don't let Nathan eat off the counters.

CORAL. You got it. Thanks, Sheila.

SHEILA. Ah hem… I should remind you, I'm also the Justice of the Peace. If you and Floyd ever get round to thinking about tying the knot. I'd be happy to do the deed.

CORAL. You never know. Maybe one day we'll take you up on that. Let us get used to being parents first. To Nathan, that is.

> *(***OCEANA*** returns with a brown paper bag containing the "to go" chowder.)*

OCEANA. Here you are! *(She sees* **SHEILA** *to the door and looks out.)* How ya doing, Larry? *(To* **CORAL***.)* What's Floyd doing out there? Running around in the snow playing with a dog?

CORAL. That's Nathan! He's not a dog. He's Floyd's and my new baby! We just adopted him!

OCEANA. You mean, after all these years, I'm an aunt?

CORAL. Looks that way!

OCEANA. Wahoo! *(She and* **CORAL** *hug.)*

> *(***MARINA*** comes down hobbling down the stairs.)*

MARINA. I knew I should have taken a sleeping pill. That mattress is full of lumps. My back is killing me. And my ankle is throbbing. I need a pain killer. You wouldn't happen to have any Vicodin would you? Mine is in my other bag at home. *(She looks around.)* Oh well, I guess a double vodka martini will have to do. What's going on? Where is everybody?

CORAL. You won't believe it. You better sit down.

MARINA. Did Pearl swim off okay?

OCEANA. Well, yes and no.

MARINA. What does that mean? Is she gone or not?

CORAL. She's gone all right.

MARINA. *(Handing a note in an envelope to* **OCEANA.***)* Here. I found this on the hall table upstairs. It's addressed to the three of us. Pearl must have written us a thank you note. Before she swam away.

OCEANA. She didn't swim away. Well, she did, but then she came back. For Nathan. They ran off together.

MARINA. Really! After we warned her? About what to expect? From *mortal* men? *(Philosophically.)* I suppose they can't help it. Men, that is. They're only *human,* after all.

OCEANA. We were warned if you recall.

MARINA. And if you recall we should have heeded to the sound advice given to us by our elders!

OCEANA. But we didn't. And neither did Pearl.

CORAL. I have a feeling that things are going to turn out different for Pearl. Better. Great, in fact.

MARINA. You? You haven't had an optimistic thought in thirty years.

CORAL. Until tonight.

MARINA. What happened tonight?

OCEANA. A lot! Let's see what she says.

> *(***OCEANA*** opens the envelope and reads the note to herself as* **FLOYD** *enters from the kitchen holding a dog leash.)*

FLOYD. Stay there, boy. I'll be right back. *(***FLOYD*** puts his arm around* **CORAL** *and they kiss.)*

MARINA. *(Reacting to the kiss and not believing her eyes — when she went for her siesta,* **FLOYD** *and* **CORAL** *still hated each other.)* My goodness! I *did* miss a lot didn't I? I must have been asleep for longer than I thought. And, what's up with the dog leash? You two aren't planning to get *kinky* in your senior years, are you?

OCEANA. Listen to this! *(Reading.)* "Dear Coral, Oceana and Toe Nail"

MARINA. Ugh! Would everyone please stop it already with "Toe Nail!"

OCEANA. Shhh! "Dear Coral, Oceana and" *(She puts out her hand to* **MARINA** *as if to gesture the third name,* **MARINA**/*Toe Nail but she doesn't say it for fear of* **MARINA** *interrupting again.)* "Thank you for sharing your stories with me. I am sorry that things didn't work out the way you hoped when you came ashore many years ago. But, that was then, and this is now, and I have to follow my heart. I love Nathan and he loves me. I offered Nathan my treasure…"

MARINA. Foolish, foolish fishgirl!!!!!

OCEANA. *(To* **MARINA**.*)* HUSH! *(Reading more animated/ excited because this is the good part.)* "I offered Nathan my treasure but he refused it."

CORAL. He *what?*

OCEANA. *(Reading.)* "Nathan told me that if he accepted my treasure he would never be able to prove to me that he loves me for me and not for my riches. After all, Nathan told me that **true love is priceless**."

MARINA. *(Sniffling at the sentiment and wiping her eyes.)* I need a tissue.

CORAL. *(Also sniffling.)* Me too!!!

OCEANA. *(Reading.)* "So, I decided since Nathan didn't want my treasure I would give it to the three of you. To repay you for sharing your kindness and wisdom, although I don't agree with your advice and have chosen not to take it. I am, after all, an adult now and can make up my own mind. So, next time you go out back, look in the large cold box where you keep the dead fish. If you look underneath the Mahi Mahi on the left, you'll find my treasure chest. My wish is that the three of you share it equally. I hope you remember me as the years go by and I wish you peace, happiness and prosperity. Love, Pearl"

MARINA. She left us her treasure! *(Dancing around but hurting her ankle in the process.)* Owwww. My foot!

CORAL. *(Jumping for joy.)* I can't believe it! We're rich! We're rich!

OCEANA. We can pay back the loan! Tell *the Captain* to shove it!

MARINA. Yeah! Where the sun don't shine!

FLOYD. Coral, I didn't know you were hard pressed for money. I'd have been happy to help you and Oceana out.

CORAL. You? Have money?

FLOYD. Yup. I'm downright loaded.

CORAL. You're kidding?

FLOYD. Nope. Started me up a social networking website a few years ago. In fact, thought it might be a way to try to find you. Called it "SeeLife." For folks who like to "See Life" – travel around and share their experiences. Post pictures. Give hotel and restaurant reviews and recommendations. That sort of thing. Was quite a hit. Sold my little company to a big internet travel company last year. Made a few million in the process.

CORAL. A few million?

FLOYD. Yeah. 'Bout twenty or thirty. Million. Don't recall. Gave half of it away. At least. To charity. Medical research. To help find a cure for what brought down Marilyn. What do I need with all that dough? Lotta women out there suffering like Marilyn did. Hope they do find a cure one day. I've always loved you, Coral. Since that day in the water. But, Marilyn was my wife for many years. I loved her too.

CORAL. I know you did. You're a good man, Floyd. Marilyn was lucky to have you. And, so am I.

FLOYD. Nah. I'm the lucky one.

OCEANA. But, Floyd! Why do you drive around in that old jalopy? And you're always complaining about the price of gas.

FLOYD. She's not a jalopy. And no matter how much money you have the price of gasoline is outrageous. I don't complain for myself. But lots of hardworking folks out there can't afford it.

OCEANA. Coral! You know what this means? We can finally afford to remodel and renovate! Maybe by the time summer comes we'll have a decent Bed & Breakfast for guests to stay when they come to the beach.

CORAL. We can even put in a swimming pool! And a hot tub!

MARINA. Hey! Wait a minute! You read the note! We share equally in the treasure. You know what that means, don't you! *(Beat.)* I'm your ***partner***!

CORAL & OCEANA. Of course you are! *(They hug her.)*

MARINA. Let's see. We can break through that wall there and make this room into a real dining room with a parlor and sitting room over there. And, I can already think of a thousand ways to decorate. This is going to be such fun!

OCEANA. It is, isn't it?

MARINA. There's just one thing though.

CORAL. What?

MARINA. As revolting as your calling me ***Toe Nail*** has been for all these years, I just cannot fathom the horror of being referred to as a "Sea Hag." We're going to have to come up with a new name for our establishment. After all, we do want this to be a respectable, upscale B&B don't we?

FLOYD. I hope you're not thinking of out pricing the hardworking folks who need a vacation. They deserve a decent place to eat and stay too you know.

MARINA. Of course they do. And, that's why, now that I'm rich again, I refuse to inflate the profit margin. Too many years of that got me absolutely nowhere.

FLOYD. Good. Glad to know you learned a lesson.

CORAL. I don't know. I kind of like Sea Hags.

OCEANA. No. I agree with Marina. It's time for a change. How about… I know! Inn of the Deep Sea Divas?

MARINA. Hmmm. I like it. That's a definite possibility.

CORAL. Deep Sea Divas. I don't know. Are we Divas?

MARINA. I don't know about you, but I definitely am. Wait! I have it!

CORAL. What?

MARINA. In honor of our benefactor: "The Pearl."

OCEANA. I love it!

CORAL. I do too! Floyd what do you think?

FLOYD. The Pearl. Sounds classy. Like the three of you. I like it.

MARINA. It's settled then!

(Dog barks.)

FLOYD. Nathan's calling me. Here I come, boy. (He exits.) Good doggie.

OCEANA. I have an idea! (She runs to the kitchen and returns with a bottle of Champagne and three glasses.) Let's have a toast!

CORAL. Where have you been hiding that?

OCEANA. Never mind! I've been saving it for a special occasion.

MARINA. Well, this is about as special as you can get.

OCEANA. To Pearl!

CORAL. And Nathan!

OCEANA. May they live happily ever after!

MARINA. Because heaven knows… (Beat.)

MARINA, OCEANA, CORAL. (They put their heads together, then in unison joyfully exclaim.) We will!!!

(They clink glasses as take a celebratory drink as the lights fade and the curtain closes.)

(blackout/curtain)

End of Play